## "Is Something Wrong With The Chowder?" Felicity Asked.

"No. It's fine. I'm not hungry."

"Clark, you did this at breakfast, too. I wish you would tell me what's wrong with my cooking."

"Nothing, except that I don't know how to eat it. I don't know which spoon to use or where to lay the silverware after I'm done with it," he said sharply.

"Are you serious?" Felicity didn't care which utensil he used; she had simply been glad to see him attack the food with a hearty appetite.

"Not everyone was raised with your advantages, you know. The finer points of etiquette weren't stressed where I just came from." He stalked toward the door.

"Listen, I spent a lot of time making this dinner. I knew that you had hardly eaten all day and I wanted to fix something nice. I shouldn't have bothered."

"No, you shouldn't have bothered. People like me aren't worth the effort."

"Someone should teach you some manners, Mr. Fielding," she said haughtily.

His gaze taunted her. "What do you expect from an ex-con?"

Dear Reader,

Season's Greetings!

This holiday season is one we associate not only with the hope for peace on earth and goodwill to all, but with love and giving. Perhaps the greatest gift is the gift of love—and that's what romance is all about.

The six Silhouette Desires this month are a special present from each author, and are for you, with love from Silhouette. In every romance, the characters must not only discover their own capacity for love, but the ability to give it fully to another human being. Sometimes that involves taking great risks— but the rewards more than compensate!

I hope you enjoy Silhouette Desire's December lineup, and that you will join us this month and every month. Capture the magic of romance—the gift of love.

Best wishes from all of us at Silhouette Books.

# CANDICE ADAMS
# A Taste of Freedom

Silhouette Desire

Published by Silhouette Books New York

**America's Publisher of Contemporary Romance**

**SILHOUETTE BOOKS**
300 East 42nd St., New York, N.Y. 10017

Copyright © 1987 by Lois Walker

ISBN: 0-373-05394-0

First Silhouette Books printing December 1987

America's Publisher of Contemporary Romance

Printed in the U.S.A.

**Books by Candice Adams**

Silhouette Desire

*Yesterday and Tomorrow* #287
*No Holding Back* #358
*A Taste of Freedom* #394

---

## CANDICE ADAMS

wrote her first romance in a motel room while on a job assignment. After the first book sold, she quit the job and devoted herself full-time to writing. She currently lives in Indiana.

# One

---

Felicity could tell the man standing in her parlor felt ill at ease. The tightness in his jaw and hooded look in his vivid gray eyes conveyed taut wariness. She wondered why.

He was clean shaven and dressed in a new gray sweatshirt and new pair of jeans. The fact he was carrying only a gym bag was not particularly unusual; many people who came to her bed and breakfast traveled light. It wasn't that he was handsome in a hard kind of way that caught at her attention. It was something else, something disturbing, that she couldn't put her finger on.

He had asked if she had a room available.

"Yes," she heard herself answering. Although she needed the money, if he really made her uneasy why hadn't she said no?

In the confines of the stately room, with its old cherry furniture and a turn-of-the-century medallion sofa, the man looked angular and restless. And he was watching her.

Smiling regally, she indicated the leather book on the writing desk. "Would you sign the guest book, please?"

He wrote *Clark Fielding* in a brisk hand and under home address he simply put *Boston*. Felicity decided not to press for more.

"Your room is at the top of the stairs, Mr. Fielding. Here's the key."

Was it her imagination or was he careful not to touch her when he accepted the key?

"The bathroom is across the hall," she added.

Nodding, he started toward the stairs.

His movements were controlled, Felicity noted. Her gaze skimmed to his lean hips, and even her wellbred background didn't stop her from appreciating the nicest male derriere she'd seen in some time.

He turned back to her. "What time is breakfast?"

Somehow he had known she was watching. She turned pink. "It's at eight."

He nodded again and disappeared out the door.

The blush—the curse of her fair skin—slowly died off her cheeks. Blushing was the one unfortunate habit her grandmother had not been able to train out of her. Felicity had been raised by her very proper Grandmother Simmons after the death of her parents in a sailing accident off the Cape. Gram put great stock in the right schools and the right people, and she had the money and social connections to follow through. From the best private school to an elaborate coming-out party, Felicity had had all the advantages.

Gram would have liked for her to marry Stewart Noyles the day after she graduated from college. But by then Felicity had developed a mind of her own. Not only was she not in love with Stewart, but she wanted to make her own way in the world.

So she had worked in an office until she saved enough money to realize her dream of moving to the house on the Cape that her parents had left her.

A distant Simmons ancestor had built the mansion outside one of the small towns on the Cape. The patriarch operated with the firm conviction a village would spring up around the house. The attitude was typical of her family's sense of superiority, Felicity thought with a dry smile. The Simmonses thought they had only to lead and the rest of the world would follow. Now the white Victorian house with its layers of gingerbread woodwork stood alone alongside the highway, grand and imposing at the edge of the sea-swept dunes. Behind the dunes and visible from the house were the everchanging blues and grays of the ocean. A cranberry bog on one side turned the landscape red in October.

A turret rose up on one side of the house and narrow windows of leaded glass perched atop the regular windows in the living and dining rooms. The staircase rising grandly in the entryway was of polished mahogany.

Felicity loved this house, and she had hit upon the perfect way to allow herself to live there. She had decided to turn it into a bed and breakfast. Grandmother had not approved.

"You, an innkeeper?" Gram had sniffed. "My dear, I don't think that's wise. I was talking with Stewart's mother just the other day at the club. Stewart is back in town, you know, and she mentioned having you over for tea while he's here and—"

Felicity interrupted with a kiss on her grandmother's withered cheek. "Gram, this is something I want to do."

"Stubborn, just like your father."

And you, Felicity had thought but remained silent.

"It's not even safe. One never knows what sort of riffraff might show up on the doorstep."

"If they don't look acceptable, I can always tell them I don't have a room available," Felicity had pointed out.

"Stubborn," Gram had repeated with strong disapproval.

Felicity had not argued; she had simply gone ahead with her plans. How could she explain that she felt a peace at the Cape that she didn't experience anywhere else? It sounded ridiculous for a twenty-eight-year-old woman to cling to memories of a time she could barely recall. The saltwater scent and the sound of the third stair creaking took her back to that innocent time when she had been cuddled by two loving parents. Back to a time when she had felt utterly safe.

Until today, she had not had any reservations about her guests. But the man who had left the room only moments earlier was the only person staying at the inn tonight. Did it bother her to be alone in the house with him?

It didn't. But she had the feeling it ought to.

Clark stood a long time in the doorway staring at the room he had just rented. Blue calico curtains hung on the window and a matching spread covered the brass bed. Tiny flowers danced on the soft beige wallpaper. An area rug with a muted rose pattern covered the hardwood floor. Slowly he bent to touch it.

He knew the woman downstairs had been unsure about him. He wondered how she would feel if she could see him rubbing his fingers back and forth through the soft wool nap of her rug. Rising, he walked to the window and placed his palms on the wide ledge. For the first time in three years he looked through a window without bars.

The backyard sloped down to sand dunes and beyond that, blue-gray water stretched to the horizon. The view was in stark contrast to the grim exercise yard he had been able to see from his cell.

The empty beach beckoned. With an odd sensation in his stomach, he realized he was actually free to go outside without permission and the escort of a guard. On the way out of the room, he paused to run work-coarsened fingers over the smooth porcelain doorknob. How different it felt from the cold steel of his cell door.

Clark was at the bottom of the steps when he encountered the woman again.

"Going for a walk?" she asked.

He nodded. Although she was not tall, she carried herself proudly, her chin tilted up at a haughty angle. Everything about her spoke of money. Even her nose was aristocratically straight. Still, he conceded that she was pretty, with smooth, fair skin and honey-blond hair pulled back into a knot. Her eyes were a deep, pure blue. It had been a long time since he had stood this close to a woman. It felt strange.

"Enjoy yourself," she said briskly.

He nodded again.

Felicity kept walking, irritated by the man's brusque silence. She had merely been trying to be friendly.

It was only since college that she had learned to be more outgoing with strangers. Gram had raised her to speak in social-register accents and to always maintain a cool dignity. All the girls at her private boarding school did. So it was a shock to Felicity when at college someone called her a snob.

Hurt, she had made an honest effort to be more outgoing. She had watched other girls who were bouncy and fun-loving and had tried to copy them, but she could not completely overcome her natural reserve. Her attempts felt strained, and she never mastered the art of letting herself go.

At least she was never rude, she thought tartly. And in the eight months she had operated the bed and breakfast, no other guest had been as uncivil to her as Clark Fielding.

Irritated, she started toward the kitchen. As she pushed through the swinging door, the sound of rapidly dripping water greeted her, sweeping aside thoughts of her guest.

Not again! The plumber had been here twice last week. Felicity could not afford to have him out again. The sad truth was the inn was barely squeaking by. During the tourist season the rooms had stayed full, but the season was months behind her now. It was late fall and guests were few and far between.

Naturally, a Simmons would never starve. But Felicity had no money of her own. Her parents had lived well beyond their means and had died in debt.

Although Gram Simmons had paid off their bills from her considerable fortune, she had resented her son's life-style and had always made it clear to Felicity that she did not intend to support her. Gram most particularly would not contribute a cent toward keeping the bed and breakfast open.

Pride and determination had kept Felicity going. On a deeper level she was also driven by a need to remain in the one place where she had known the greatest security. But at the moment she was not sure how much longer she could manage to hang on.

Leaving the dripping water behind, she pulled on a heavy hand-knit sweater and crossed the wide yard to the road. Walking beneath the big oak tree and hearing the surf in the background calmed her.

But her calm was shaken again when she opened the mail box. Three bills awaited her. Solemnly, she tore open the electric bill. Her spirits sank. It alone would clean her out. That left no money with which to pay the plumber or the gardener.

Dispirited, she trudged back across the yard to the front steps, hugging herself against a sudden gust of November wind. She pondered how to raise enough money to stay afloat until tourist season began again next summer.

A part-time job was out of the question because she had to be here if someone stopped to rent a room. Besides, what kind of work could she do on the Cape? Her skills were mainly drawing-room accomplishments. As a child she had actually studied deportment—and ballet. Then there had been those endless hours of classical piano lessons.

Piano. Halting on the top step of the wooden wraparound porch, she stared through the window at the baby grand in the parlor. She could give lessons. Brightening, she realized she might also give painting lessons.

"Hello, Felicity."

Startled, she turned to see Ralph Bennett coming up the stairs.

"Time to check the filter on that furnace," he announced cheerfully.

She blinked. "Again?"

The balding man smiled indulgently. "You don't want it clogging up and running up your fuel bill. No need to show me where it is. I know my way." With a parting wave, he entered the house.

Dispirited, Felicity followed slowly. Ralph's was one more bill she would have to pay. As she stood in the hallway, her hand on the polished banister, the door opened again, and Clark Fielding entered.

It struck her that he moved with a surprising lack of noise for a man his size. He must be six feet tall, but he was so quiet he could have been a cat burglar.

His eyes met hers. Since they were staring right at each other, she felt obliged to say something. "Did you have a good walk?" If she was crisp, it was because he had not gone out of his way to show any friendliness.

"Fine," he said tersely, passing her on his way to the stairs. Suddenly, a door slammed in the basement and he froze. "What's that?" he demanded tightly.

"A man looking at the furnace." She watched the tensed muscles relax. "Is something wrong, Mr. Fielding?"

"No." Without another word, he mounted the stairs.

Again Felicity found herself staring after him. Only this time her doubts about him were stronger. Why would anyone be so jumpy about a noise?

Once Ralph Bennett left, she would be alone in the house with Clark Fielding. In less than two hours it would be dark. Did she want to be alone with this man? On the other hand, she had never asked a guest to leave before.

"Maybe I'm making a mountain out of a molehill," she murmured aloud.

Yet Gram's oft-repeated warning, "It's better to prevent an unpleasant situation from occurring than try to get yourself out of it later," was lodged firmly in her mind. If she was going to ask her guest to leave, she had to do it now.

Taking a breath deep enough to draw her back up straight, she marched upstairs and knocked on his door. As always when confronted with an unpleasant task, she fell back on excessive dignity.

Clark Fielding opened his door.

With the hauteur of a village schoolmistress, she said, "I must speak with you."

He inclined his head warily. "Go ahead."

"I regret to say this, but I'm uneasy about you. Perhaps it would be better if you rented another room for the night. There are plenty available on the Cape. Naturally, I shall refund your money." She kept her eye firmly trained on a spot on the wall while she delivered her piece.

Clark glanced around at the wall, then back at her. "Are you talking to me?"

"Of course I am."

"Then look at me."

She did. His gray eyes were inscrutable and no muscle moved in his face. Yet he stood ramrod straight, staring her down in a way that actually took some of the starch out of her.

"Tell me why you want me to leave."

"You act—" She lifted her chin higher, determined not to be intimidated. "There's something different about you."

He nodded slowly, his eyes never leaving her. "Yes, there is. I just got out of prison."

Felicity flinched. This was even worse than she had thought.

"I'm not dangerous," he continued in a flinty, uncompromising voice, "but if you want me to go, I will."

"Th-that might be best." Good heavens, no Simmons had stuttered since descending from the *May-*

*flower*. But surely none had been confronted with a situation like this, she reasoned.

Turning away, he picked up the gym bag. "You'll have to drive me into town. I got off the bus out front but I guess it doesn't run by again until tomorrow."

"I'll be glad to drive you." Was that her voice that sounded so fluttery? A whole spectrum of emotions juggled inside her. One of them was alarm. Another was sympathy. Whatever he had done, he had been punished for it. Today might be his first day of freedom after months or years of dehumanizing experiences in prison.

She tried for a soothing tone. "I don't mean to be unkind. I hope you understand my position."

He laughed harshly. "Spare me, lady. Just take me into town."

They left the house in silence and got into her European luxury car. It had been a gift from Gram, with the stipulation she was not allowed to trade it for money to support the inn. Felicity didn't think she could part with it anyway. She loved this car.

Turning the ignition key, she pulled out of the drive.

The deadly silence between them made her uncomfortable. It didn't help matters when she came up behind an impossibly slow car, and she couldn't find a place to pass.

The autumn sky had turned a threatening charcoal color and the wind had picked up considerably.

November was always a chancy time on the Cape, with heavy rains graying the skies and harsh winds blowing down from the northeast. Too late, Felicity remembered storm warnings and realized she was driving right into bad weather.

Just then a hard blast of wind buffeted the little car. As she struggled to regain control, a semi truck shot by and sent the car careening toward the shoulder. For a wild instant, she thought she was going to run off the road and hit a tree.

Shaken, she jerked the wheel hard. Rocks scattered and pelted the side of the car as she plowed to a stop on the narrow shoulder. Wind continued to rock the car. In the rearview mirror she saw her ashen reflection.

After a moment's silence, he demanded, "Are we going to sit here all day?"

Felicity stiffened. The absolute gall of the man. "I cannot possibly drive yet. I need time to collect myself."

"Then I'll drive," he said.

She stared at him, taking in his dark hair and the hard set of his jaw. No one else had ever driven her expensive car. "You must be joking."

A glint of cold amusement played in his eyes. "If you're afraid to let me behind the wheel because you think I went to prison for kidnapping, I didn't. Besides, I damn sure wouldn't kidnap anyone who's as much trouble as you."

She counted to ten, the way Gram had taught her as a child, before saying levelly, "This is not very pleasant for either of us."

"You got that right, lady."

They were alone at the side of the deserted road. If he wanted to harm her, she supposed he would have done it by now. Suddenly, she felt more dog tired and anxious to be back home than frightened of him. Besides, if they continued driving, they would be heading into the worst of the storm.

"We're nine miles from town and only two from my house," she said. "It would probably be the safest course to go back there."

His jawline tightened again. "And have you worry that I'll murder you in your sleep? No, thanks."

She gestured wearily toward the road. "The wind is too treacherous. Would you rather dread that you're going to get killed out here?" Without waiting for a reply, she turned the car around.

As they lapsed into silence again, Felicity wondered what he was thinking.

She would have been surprised to know, as the coupe sped along the twisting roads, that Clark was remembering the last time he had been inside a private car. It had been a battered blue Chevy, and the day had been one of those frigid ones that makes a Boston man think of becoming a Florida man.

He had just returned home from his construction job when the phone rang.

"I need you to do me a favor," his brother Larry began without preamble. "Tonight."

"Larry, can it wait? I'm tired. I want to sit down with a beer and watch the fights."

"Man, I need you!"

Instantly, he tensed. "What's wrong? Are you in trouble again?"

"No, but you gotta do this for me. I need a ride tonight. Pick me up at the McGill warehouse. South door at midnight."

"What the hell are you going to be doing there?"

"Just be there!" Larry hung up.

Clark damn sure would be there. His kid brother was up to no good, and he intended to stop it. Larry had been in enough trouble already. All those years of poverty had made him hell-bent on getting rich quick. He could never hold a job because he was always looking for the easy angle.

Perhaps if someone had been there to discipline Larry when he was a child, he would have turned out differently. But their father had abandoned the family after Larry was born and had not been heard from again. Their mother had worked two jobs to make ends meet. When she came home from the night shift of waitressing, she was too tired to fight with her sons. So they had pretty much raised themselves.

Clark had been two years older and infinitely more responsible. When he was nine, his mother put him in charge in her absence.

He could see her now, the lines of worry grooved deep in her face as she sat on the ratty living-room sofa and chain-smoked.

"I can't afford to hire no baby-sitter no longer, honey. They're going to throw us out of this place if I miss another rent payment. You're going to have to be the man of the house and take care of Larry when I'm at work."

Clark had tried. But Larry had a penchant for finding the wrong crowd—which wasn't hard to do in the tough Boston neighborhood they lived in. By the time Larry was fourteen, he had been picked up by the police half a dozen times.

Then things got tougher financially. Their mother was laid off. Looking back, Clark realized that was when she gave up. What began as an occasional drink soon became an every-night occurrence. She got a new job but began missing work. When they fired her, she didn't bother to look for another.

Clark was sixteen at the time, and he did what he had to. He quit school, lied about his age and got hired doing backbreaking construction work. The men he worked with were a hard crowd, and he soon became hardened as well. He didn't start fights, but he didn't shy away from them either.

The only time he was soft was with Larry and his mother. Even then he hid behind a gruff exterior. But he couldn't bring himself to beat the meanness out of his kid brother, even though that was the way some of his fellow workers handled their children.

If Clark had gotten physical back then, would it have saved his own skin as well as Larry's later? He didn't know.

All he knew was when he showed up at the warehouse that night, Larry jumped in shouting "Drive!"

"What's going on?"

"Just drive! The damned alarm is going off. The police will be here any minute."

Clark stabbed his foot to the floor, and the car skidded forward on the ice. Gripping the wheel with nervous fingers, he whipped the car around a corner and headed away from the water. "Larry, what did you do?"

His brother was looking frantically out the back window. "Damn! They're coming!"

The memory remained vivid three years later. The sirens, Clark's own panicked driving until he was boxed in by police cars, then the trial and finally prison.

He had entered prison protesting his innocence. How naive he had been, he thought with a self-mocking smile. Every man there claimed to have been "framed." After a while, he realized it was hopeless trying to convince anyone he was a victim of circumstances. He had become hard and stoic and did his time without any more idiotic declarations of innocence. Of course he was bitter at the injustice, but he didn't dwell on it. Nothing could change the way things were.

Clark came out of his reverie just as the woman drove into the yard. Picking up his gym bag, he entered the house and went directly up to the blue room. She didn't want him here, and tomorrow he would leave. But for the moment he was going to enjoy his first night's sleep in three years in a decent bed.

# Two

———

Felicity slept surprisingly well that night. By seven the next morning, she was downstairs in the kitchen. Her honey-blond hair was pulled back into a ponytail that swished against her bare neck. Her striped jeans and blue velour top felt soft and warm against her skin on this nippy November day.

The big kitchen looked very much like it had at the turn of the century. It contained an old sink with porcelain knobs and high pine cabinets that reached to the ceiling. The stove and refrigerator were old white appliances from the fifties. Only the wallpaper with its cheery yellow flowers was new. Felicity intended to have the whole room modernized when she had the money.

While the bacon fried, she checked the blueberry muffins in the oven. Once everything was done, she covered the food to keep it warm, poured a cup of coffee and carried it into the dining room. At the table, she opened the paper and took a sip of the steaming coffee.

"Good morning."

She jumped at the sound of a man's voice behind her. Hot coffee sloshed over her hands and onto the white damask tablecloth. Flustered, she demanded, "Don't you *ever* make noise when you walk?"

"I didn't mean to scare you."

Felicity mopped at the coffee with a cloth napkin. "Well, you did. If this keeps up, I'll have to tie a bell around your neck." Belatedly mindful that he *was* a paying guest, she said quietly, "I'll bring in your breakfast."

She escaped to the kitchen and filled two plates with food, wondering why Clark Fielding made her so uneasy. She had slept safely enough last night. Yet looking at those impenetrable steel-gray eyes still made her jittery.

She returned to the dining room, carrying a wooden tray laden with full plates for both of them as well as jelly and butter in crystal dishes and real silver utensils.

She handed him his plate. Before she could even sit down, Clark had scooped up several blueberry muffins and began lathering butter on them.

Carefully placing her napkin in her lap, she daintily broke a piece off her muffin, buttered the tiny portion and placed her knife on the edge of the plate.

Across the table, Clark paused, then picked up his knife from the table and laid it on his plate. After a moment's hesitation, he pushed back his chair and rose.

She looked at his full plate. Having had cooking lessons from one of the finest chefs in Boston, she prided herself on her culinary skills. Usually she was complimented on her food. At least no one had ever walked away from it before. Then why had Clark Fielding? Judging from the way he had initially attacked the food, he was quite hungry.

"Is something wrong with the food, Mr. Fielding?"

"No. I have to pack."

Felicity looked up into unwavering gray eyes. "You have plenty of time to eat, Mr. Fielding. The bus won't be here for over five hours."

Shrugging, he started from the room.

He was almost to the door, oblivious to her narrowed gaze on his back, when she heard the sound of gushing water. "Oh, no!" Flinging aside her napkin, she ran into the kitchen.

Clark followed.

Water shot from the tap in an angry stream, hitting the porcelain surface of the sink and spraying upward. She ran across the room and vainly turned the faucet handles. The water continued to pour out.

"Call the plumber," she shouted and then hurried to the wall phone to do it herself.

While she ripped through her address book in search of the plumber's phone number, she had a distracted impression of Clark opening the doors below the sink and calmly bending to look inside.

Suddenly the room was silent.

She paused in the act of dialing. "What did you do?"

"Turned the water off. There's a shutoff valve underneath." He was on his knees now in front of the open doors studying the pipes.

"A shutoff valve?" Her hand dropped away from the phone.

"Yes, but it has to be turned on again for the water to work. You'll have to fix whatever caused the problem. A bad washer, I'd say."

"So I still need a plumber," she said in defeat. She had not paid his last bill, and she had no idea how she would afford this one.

"Got a pipe wrench?" Clark asked.

"What does one look like?"

He shot her a suspicious glance. "Are you serious?"

"I most certainly am." Why did he seem so surprised? A knowledge of wrenches was not the sort of thing girls at finishing school were taught. "There are some tools in the basement that were Daddy's."

Pushing himself off his knees, he mumbled, "Let's see if Daddy knew what a pipe wrench was."

Felicity led him down into the basement, moving ahead to pull the dangling string that turned on the lights. "Over here above the workbench."

Clark picked up several tools from the collection hanging on the wall. "Maybe we can do something with these."

Feeling useless, she followed him up the steps into the kitchen. Within minutes, he had dismantled the pipe system under the cabinet.

Maybe he could find the problem and she wouldn't have to pay a plumber, she thought hopefully. But as her gaze skimmed the collection of metal accumulating on the red tile floor, a new worry assaulted her. "You *do* know how to put this back together, don't you?"

"No, I was hoping you would remember."

"Me! I—" Felicity broke off when she realized he was grinning up at her. It was the first time she had seen him smile. Bemused, she reflected he ought to do it more often. He looked terribly appealing with a teasing light in those fascinating gray eyes and the small trace of a dimple in his left cheek.

Turning away, he ducked back under the sink. "Whoever does your plumbing has things in a hell of a mess. He's got eighth-inch pipe going into half-inch. Eighth-inch is way too small for a line like this. The water pressure must be screwed up completely. I'm going to need some new pieces to straighten things out."

As the innkeeper, Felicity knew she should object to a guest spending his time on her problem. But she was too grateful to do more than murmur, "I'll get a sheet of paper and write down what you need."

Picking up the pad from the antique pine desk in the corner of the kitchen, she wrote while he rattled off a list.

Finally he rose, pulled a paper towel from the holder and wiped his hands. "Let's go."

She was not used to being ordered around. For an instant, her Simmons dignity rebelled, and she remained motionless.

He glanced back at her. "What's wrong?"

"You could at least say *please*." As soon as the words were out, she felt petty and ridiculous. For pete's sake, the man was doing her a favor. At times like this she wished she had not had etiquette drilled so deeply into her that she put unnecessary weight on it.

But Clark Fielding didn't seem affronted. Instead, he paused. "Please," he said, weighing the word carefully as if to determine how it sounded.

"I'll get my purse and car keys," she said.

On the way to town, Felicity was too preoccupied to notice the scrubgrass-covered dunes and the sea gulls wheeling above a lonely lighthouse. Even the lead-gray sky that threatened more rain made no impression on her.

She was thinking about the man beside her and wondering how often the inmates in prison had said "please" to him or to anyone else. No wonder Clark Fielding spoke it as if it were a foreign word.

They were at the edge of the village now, beside the first of the low-crouching shingled houses so indicative of the Cape style. She glanced over at him, wondering if he thought of her as full of pompous airs and graces. Considering he was doing her a favor by fixing her broken faucet, she wondered why he hadn't told her to go to hell when she'd demanded her "please." The very least she could do was apologize.

"I'm sorry," she said with uncustomary humility.

He glanced over at her. "Why?"

"I shouldn't have acted so—so snobbish back at the house. It was enough that you were helping me. It was wrong to demand that you treat me like the queen."

"I figure you're used to being treated like a queen," he said matter-of-factly.

Stung, and trying not to show it, she steered the car into a parking place in front of the old clapboard hardware store at the edge of the sleepy downtown and turned to him.

"What makes you say that?" she asked stiffly.

"Everything about you says Rich Girl. Rich people get treated better than slobs like me." Brittle humor and bitterness put an edge in his voice.

"I'm *not* rich."

His eyebrows went up in disbelief.

"Well, there is some money in the family," she conceded reluctantly.

Wordlessly, letting his sardonic expression say it all, he got out of the car and walked into the store.

Felicity waited outside, staring at the Greek revival, Victorian Gothic and Italianate houses facing the ribbon of road that ran down Main Street and then out of town to become the main highway along the Cape. The impressive old houses stood as reminders of the sea captains who had struck it rich in fishing, whaling and the China trade. Usually, Felicity could find quiet satisfaction in observing the varying architectural styles. Today, all she could think about was the infuriating man inside the store.

But the autumn air was cold, and she was wearing only a flannel shirt. Comfort won over wounded pride, and she went inside to wait in the dusky store while he made his selections from an assortment of bins.

Standing by the front door, she noted the rugged grace in his brisk stride. The only other customer in the store, a young woman, was also watching Clark, Felicity realized. It stood to reason. He had an attractive, masculine body and dark good looks.

Had there been a woman in his life before he went to prison? Evidently there was not one now. From out of nowhere the realization hit Felicity that Clark Fielding had not had a woman in a very long time. She didn't usually speculate on other people's private lives, but then she didn't often spend time with a virile, sexy man just out of prison.

Hoping he couldn't read her thoughts, she made her face a cool mask as he walked toward her.

"I think this is everything." He put a collection of pipes on the scarred wooden counter.

The crusty old proprietor began punching numbers into a calculator. "That's $39.87," he announced.

Clark turned to her.

With a start, Felicity realized she didn't have the money. She could not even write a check because she didn't have enough in the bank to cover it. And she was uncomfortably aware both men were staring at her. One of Gram's early lessons had been to avoid embarrassing oneself in public at all costs.

"Just a minute, please," Felicity said pleasantly, "I thought of one other thing we need. Clark, could you help me get it?"

Pivoting with ballerina ease, she walked to the back of the store. He followed.

"I don't have any money," she said in a low voice.

Clark shot an exasperated look at the pressed tin ceiling. "Can we continue this discussion in the car? Whether you have money or your family does is irrelevant. Let's just pay and get out of here."

Drawing a deep breath, she tried again. "I don't have enough to pay the bill." Or even to invest much in the bubble-gum machine inside the door, she thought unhappily.

His gray eyes widened in astonishment.

"I didn't realize it would cost so much and—" Swallowing a mouthful of pride, she continued humbly, "If you could pay, I would appreciate it. Naturally, I will reimburse you."

Rough amusement quirked at his mouth. The dimple in his left cheek showed to full advantage. "I wish all the guys who've tried to sponge money off me for the past three years could see this."

Felicity blinked. Sponge!

"Come on. I'll settle the bill, and we can sort this out later." Grabbing her arm, he headed for the front of the store.

She was not used to being manhandled, but she was hardly in a position to take offense at his actions. With all the dignity she could muster, she followed.

Once they had paid and left the store, Clark stepped to the driver's side of her car. Felicity thought he intended to open the door for her. Instead, he reverently stroked the side of the expensive forest-green automobile, then ventured a sideways glance at her.

"I don't suppose you'd let me drive?"

Repressing a sigh, she looked at him. He was a virtual stranger, this man with the thick dark hair, muscled chest and long legs. But she owed him. Under the circumstances, she could not very well refuse. Wordlessly she handed him the keys and walked around to the passenger's side, trying not to dwell on what Gram Simmons would say if she could see this.

Clark put the car into reverse and eased it out of the parking space. He handled the floor gearshift with skill, she noted gratefully and relaxed a little. How long had it been since he'd driven? she wondered.

Normally, a lady didn't pry, but this *was* a rather unusual situation. "When did you get out of prison?"

"Yesterday."

She looked over at his impassive face. "And you didn't want to go directly home?"

"Nothing there," he said shortly.

"But surely you have some family," she persisted.

"A brother in prison. A mother in an institution. That's it."

Felicity sat silently. Yesterday, she had felt guilty about asking him to leave. Now she felt like a complete boor. But if he was thinking along those lines, he didn't show it. In fact, he seemed totally absorbed in driving the car. One large hand lingered on the wooden shift knob, and the other held the steering wheel with a grip that was both firm and loving. Even the harsh lines of his face had softened slightly.

He had a nice profile, with long lashes and a clean-shaven jaw. His hands were rough-textured and callused, Felicity noticed. The men she knew all had soft hands except for an occasional blister from playing racquetball. Yet it appealed to her to know he had used his hands for manual labor.

"It's going to rain some more," he said flatly.

She looked out the window at the lowering sky and the rusty brown salt marsh beneath it. "It looks rather like El Greco's *View of Toledo*, don't you think?"

He glanced over at her quizzically. "View of what?"

"Toledo. Surely you've seen the painting. It's very famous."

"I'm afraid I don't know much about art," he snapped and turned his attention back to the road.

Subdued, Felicity fell back into silence. She had not meant to make him feel uneducated. Somehow she seemed to always say the wrong thing to him.

Fifteen minutes later, Clark pulled into her yard and silently handed her the keys.

Emerging from the car, he went directly to the kitchen to begin work, refusing her offer of a sandwich at lunchtime and working straight through.

It was necessary to make another trip to the hardware store because some of the pipes were rusted together and fell apart when he tried to separate them. Felicity went along but she let him drive. He derived so much pleasure from it, it seemed the least she could do.

When they returned to the house, she busied herself in the parlor calling friends to put the word out she was interested in giving piano lessons. Always, though, she kept an ear toward the kitchen.

Clark Fielding might not have a private-school finish, but those sensual eyes and that dimple when he smiled were having an effect on her. She made more trips to the kitchen than were strictly necessary, pulled toward him by an undertow she couldn't explain. Was it because he had done things and been places so far outside her realm of experience that she found him so compelling? That must be it. What other attraction could she feel toward a man who had been in prison?

Yet, for a brief moment, she faced the disturbing thought it was not Clark's background that bothered her but the lean efficiency of his body and the rugged handsomeness of his face. He was so very male and she was not used to that.

It was some time later when he finally straightened and shut the cabinet doors. "Done."

Felicity glanced over from checking supplies in the cupboards.

"I'd better wash up and get out to the road so I don't miss the bus."

She flashed a guilty look at the clock. "I'm afraid the bus went an hour ago." Quickly, she added, "Of course you can stay tonight free. And I won't charge for last night either. You've done so much work, I owe you at least that. And, as I said earlier, I'll repay what I borrowed from you."

"Yes, you will," he said in a maddeningly positive tone and left the room.

She heard him moving about upstairs and then the sound of water running while he took a shower. Suddenly she had a paralyzing vision of water cascading over his naked torso. It was an image so powerful it made her knees weak. Swallowing hard, she swept the thought aside and forced herself to prepare dinner.

Ordinarily, guests at the bed and breakfast were entitled to only breakfast. But these were not ordinary circumstances. Without a car, Clark couldn't get into town to buy his own dinner, so he would be eating with her. By the time she had the food on the table and was seated across from him, she had regained her cool composure.

"I hope you like clam chowder," she said with a very proper smile.

"Yeah." He tilted the bowl forward, picked up his teaspoon and began to take quick, hungry mouthfuls.

It was not the way men ate at the Ritz-Carlton, but she didn't mind at all. Selecting her soup spoon, she took a dainty sip from the side of the spoon.

She saw him pause. Then, with an abrupt motion, he pushed his bowl aside.

"Is something wrong with the chowder?" she asked.

"No. It's fine. I'm not hungry."

Wounded vanity—after all, she prided herself on being an excellent cook—and exasperation got the better of her. The fact he had started to eat as if he were ravenous and now was willing to go without food added to her irritation. "You did this at breakfast, too. I wish you would tell me what's wrong with my cooking."

"Nothing, except that I don't know how to eat it."

Confused, she stared at him. "I don't understand."

"I don't know which spoon to use or where to lay the silverware after I'm done with it," he said sharply.

She blinked. "Are you serious?" True, he had been using the wrong spoon, but she didn't care which utensil he used. She had simply been glad to see him attack the food with a hearty appetite, especially after he had done so much for her today.

He slammed his chair back. "Not everyone was raised with your advantages, you know. The finer points of etiquette weren't stressed in prison, either." He stalked toward the door.

For a moment, Felicity sat dumbfounded. Then she jumped up and followed, twisting her linen napkin into a tight ball between her fingers. "Before you walk out of here, I want to tell you something. I spent a lot of time making this dinner. I knew that you had hardly eaten all day, and I wanted to fix something nice. I wish I hadn't bothered," she concluded hotly. She could feel the blush rising on her cheeks as he turned at the foot of the stairs and glared at her.

"No, you shouldn't have bothered. People like me aren't worth the effort."

Indignantly, she stared at him. Men never talked to her this way. "Someone should teach you some manners, Mr. Fielding," she said haughtily. "It's rude to keep walking away after I've gone to the trouble to cook. It simply isn't done."

His gaze taunted her. "What can you expect from an ex-con?"

"I expect the same consideration as from anyone else," she countered.

That seemed to take him aback. He was silent as he frowned. Quietly, he said, "Maybe you're right."

Felicity knew she was right, but she hadn't expected him to agree.

He nodded. "Let's go eat."

His abrupt about-face threw her off stride; Felicity remained in the hall.

"What are you waiting for? The soup is getting cold."

She started back into the dining room, shaking her head as she went. One thing was certain: things had not been boring since Clark Fielding's arrival. Still, it was all to the good he would be leaving tomorrow. So why did she feel an odd sense of dissatisfaction?

"Felicity?"

She looked across the table at him.

"You were right when you said someone should teach me manners." He spoke slowly, as if each word cost him an effort of will. "There are a lot of things I want to learn. Need to learn," he added heavily. "I went to college in prison. In a month I'm going to start working with a computer company in Boston." He stopped, then cleared his throat uncomfortably.

"Yes?" she prompted.

"Where I grew up, I didn't have much chance to learn the little niceties of life. But it's important to know certain things to get along among civilized people." He looked toward a hunting print hanging over the white marble fireplace, then at the elegant Bavarian crystal in the china cabinet. He seemed to look everywhere but at her. "I don't want to be a rough ex-con all my life. I don't want to feel awkward and out of place. You know the right way of doing things. I'd pay to learn."

Startled by his request, she spoke without thinking. "Surely you don't mean you want me to teach you how to act in polite society? I really don't think—"

He cut her off. "It was just an idea. Forget it."

She knew her rejection had hurt his feelings. And why was she saying no? Hadn't she spent part of the day telephoning people and offering her services as a piano tutor? Teaching manners wouldn't be any harder. Besides, Clark wanted to learn, which was probably more than could be said for the ten-year-olds who might be sent over to warm her piano bench. Still, there were aspects of the idea that bothered her.

"If I were to agree, would you live here?" she asked carefully.

"I hadn't really thought it out. But, yeah, I guess I would. It would only be for two or three weeks. Then I need to find a place to live in Boston before my job starts."

Two weeks with a rent-paying guest *and* a student. It could bring in money she needed badly. That fact outweighed her hesitation about the unsettling effect he had on her. "Very well. I'll do it."

He cast a skeptical glance her way, as if he were no longer sure he wished her to. "I don't want to be a charity case."

"You're not. My reasons are, frankly, selfish. This is the off-season, and I could use the money." Besides, it would be a challenge. A smile crept over her face. "By the time I'm through with you, you'll be able to pass for a Boston blue blood."

Already she was looking him over speculatively, imagining him wearing a proper suit instead of a sweatshirt and jeans. She had good material to work with. The man was easy to look at and not a little sexy. Under her schooling, she would develop him into a courtly, urbane gentleman.

# Three

---

The next morning Felicity was awakened by the sound of the front door closing. Pulling a robe over her long nightgown, she walked barefooted across the thick ivory Aubusson rug to the window.

Clark was in the front yard. Through the branches of the oak, she saw him doing stretching exercises. Then he jogged off down the road. With his long legs moving powerfully, he soon attained a strong, fluid motion. Watching the energy behind each step, Felicity found it impossible to imagine him ever being caged.

He had told her he had not kidnapped anyone. What crime had he committed? she wondered. Surprisingly, she didn't feel afraid of him because he had been in prison. But there were other things about him that created an uneasy tension between them. Her instincts told her it had to do with the fact he was a virile man who had been away from women for a long time. Needs and urges that had been pushed to the side were free to surface again.

Not that he had been forward with her. On the contrary, he took great care not to get within touching distance. If they passed in the hall, he moved over farther than necessary. But he couldn't change the fact he radiated masculine sensuality. While he may have been forced to forgo pleasure during his years in prison, her woman's intuition told her he had experience in the field.

As she crossed the rug again, Felicity reflected that her own background in the sexual arena was limited. It was not that she disliked men, but her haughty bearing kept them at arm's length. Ironically, many men mistook her aloofness for the world-weariness of a woman with vast experience.

They would be surprised to know how insecure she was about her own desirability. Men treated her with reverence. She sometimes wondered if she would be able to inspire desire in the right man or if there was something missing in her personality that would prevent her from ever knowing true passion. But it was not a subject she permitted herself to dwell on.

"There's work to be done," she lectured aloud.

She was downstairs fixing coffee when Clark returned; she heard the shower running overhead. A few minutes later, he appeared in the kitchen. His cheeks were flushed from jogging. His eyelashes were wet and stuck together with water, making his gray eyes bright and lively. His plaid shirt and jeans fitted over hard, sinewy lines.

Felicity averted her glance. A Simmons did not ogle an attractive man, even one sexy enough to make the air seem charged.

She found a pleasant, neutral tone of voice and asked, "Did you have a good run?"

"Yeah." He opened the refrigerator, pulled out a carton of milk and started to drink from it.

She stared.

Lowering the carton, he grinned ruefully. "Sorry. I guess Etiquette Rule Number One is not to drink out of the carton."

"It is considered better form to use a glass." She handed him one. "In fact, we might as well start our lessons right now. In the library." Once things were on a firm teacher-pupil footing, she would get over this ridiculous notion of feeling overwhelmed by his male appeal.

He poured the milk, downed it in two swallows and set the glass aside. "Ready."

Felicity led the way across the hall bright with colors coming through a stained-glass window on the stair landing. She entered a room at the easternmost end of the house. With curved glass in the windows and a cozy turret, it had once been a sitting room. Some ancestor had installed oak bookcases along with brass reading lamps and library tables. Now it was considered the library.

"We'll start with books on art and music. I have some excellent ones you can read." Finger to her lips, she pondered the selection of leather-bound volumes. The Simmonses had always been strong supporters of the arts, and there was a large collection of books to prove it. "Here's a good book on the Impressionists. And a nice one on Picasso's early period."

Frowning, Clark looked at the thick art books. "I want to learn manners, not how to paint."

"Being well-rounded is essential to being a Renaissance man," she insisted. All the men she knew had a knowledge of music, opera and art. "You can sit at this table."

He obeyed without enthusiasm.

"You need some light," she murmured, bending over him to turn on a Tiffany lamp. Her hand brushed against his shoulder. It was an insignificant touch and he seemed to take no notice. But she did. Her fingers still tingled as she moved quickly away and she left him to his studies.

Three hours later, Felicity returned to check Clark's progress.

He was sitting at the oak table, his long legs stretched straight out in front of him and his chin propped in his left hand. He was staring outside.

"How are we doing?" she asked brightly.

"Have you noticed the drainage at this corner is toward the house? You're going to have to reslope the yard or you'll be getting water in the basement."

Her gaze went to the window. She was already getting water in the basement, but they could discuss that later. At the moment, she meant to keep him on the subject.

"I cannot teach you about the finer things in life if you are not going to concentrate. Did you do any reading at all?"

He pulled his attention back to the books. "I glanced through them. Some of the pictures are nice. This is a pretty one."

His work-roughened hands traced across a delicate reproduction of a woman and child in a green field with red poppies. It was a Monet, and one of her favorites. Felicity was surprised to find how pleased she was that he had picked it.

"It's important to have an understanding of art," she said briskly enough to cover her reaction. "During meals, we'll discuss what you've learned each day. I'll also put on classical music at dinner so you can begin to develop an appreciation for it.

"And I'll prepare a variety of meals so that you may become familiar with elegant dishes and the utensils to use with them." Felicity ticked the items off on long, slender fingers. He looked so somber, she gave him a quick, professorial smile of reassurance. "It won't be so bad."

The smile he returned was startling in its warmth and richness. "I really appreciate all you're doing for me," he said.

Her inclination was to beam at him, but she did not. Keep this impersonal, she reminded herself sternly. "You're most welcome," she said with crisp efficiency.

His smile died.

"I'll see you at dinner."

He nodded coolly.

As she left the room, she knew she had pushed him away. But it was better that he not know he made her feel uncertain and off balance. And much too womanly.

Over the next two days Clark learned quickly. He asked some perceptive questions about art during dinner and easily picked up correct silverware usage.

She was feeling very encouraged when she went into the parlor on Friday night. Clark was already sitting in front of the television on the brocade divan. His feet were propped up on a dainty, needle-pointed footstool and he held a beer in his left hand.

"I taped this week's episode of *Masterpiece Theater*," she said. "I thought we could watch it now." In fact, she had been looking forward to spending a quiet evening watching a fine performance with him.

He didn't look at her. "I planned to watch the fights tonight."

"You mean *boxing*?" Surely not. It was such a thoroughly repugnant sport that no one could possibly enjoy it.

"Yeah, boxing," he said defiantly.

She paused, then began tactfully, "I think your education would be better served by watching something else."

When he didn't dispute that, she changed the channel. For the next hour, they sat five feet away from each other, he on the divan and she on a Regency-striped chair and watched an episode of *Pride and Prejudice*. She sat spellbound, savoring every nuance of the performance. When it was over, she turned the television off with a smile of satisfaction.

"Well, what did you think of that?" she asked.

"It was a bore. Didn't those people ever do anything but talk?"

"It's a comedy of manners," she explained patiently. "The beauty of Jane Austen's works is in her subtleties."

He leaned forward and changed the channel. "Good, the fights aren't over yet."

"Don't you want to discuss what you just watched?" she persisted.

He threw an impatient glance in her direction. "Listen, it's Friday night. Give me time off for good behavior."

Felicity left the room with her chin lifted proudly. She had not considered it a chore to watch a production of a fine piece of literature. In fact, the tender story always pulled strings inside her. She suffered along with Elizabeth while the proud Darcy kept his feelings of love concealed.

From the parlor, she heard, "Looks like he's down for the count, folks."

She went upstairs to read.

Felicity's word-of-mouth campaign that she was interested in teaching piano paid off. By the end of the weekend, she had signed up four students. Between them and Clark, her finances were improving.

Sunday night, a storm moved through. November was like that. Heavy rains often grayed the skies and the winds blew hard enough to push fog in over the dunes. Rain came frequently, driving down with relentless force.

She awoke Monday morning to find water running down the outside wall of the enclosed back porch off the kitchen, leaving a rusty stain on the white railroad siding. Dismayed, she dialed the first number under "Roofing" in the phone book and asked the man to come and fix the leak.

By the time Clark returned from his jogging and had showered, the workman was outside surveying the damage.

Clark joined Felicity in the dining room where she sat figuring bills at one end of the oval table. He sat down and sipped coffee from a small flowered teacup that made his big hand look even bigger.

"Whose truck is that out front?" he asked.

"A man's here to repair the roof."

"What's wrong with it?"

She had only added up half the monthly bills and already she was in the red. To make matters worse, Clark had made her lose her place. Frustration put an edge in her voice. "It leaked last night on the back porch."

"Where?" he asked calmly.

"What?"

"Where did the water come in?"

"Down the sides of the wall," she said shortly. What difference could it possibly make? Water was water and it had to be stopped. She began to add the figures again.

"Do you call in a repairman every time you have a minor problem?"

She stiffened. "I don't consider that minor."

"It's probably only leaves backing up in the gutter causing the problem. Anyone could take care of that. I'm surprised you didn't look at it yourself first." Rising, he carried his empty cup into the kitchen. Then she heard him go up to his room.

Who did he think he was criticizing her? Pushing the checkbook aside, she ran her hands wearily over her cheeks. It was pointless to be angry at Clark. Maybe he hadn't been tactful, but there might be some truth in what he had said.

Because her grandmother had always called in workmen when something was amiss, Felicity had grown up thinking that was the way problems were handled. But the sad truth was Gram could afford to hire workers, and she could not.

Another glance at the checkbook galvanized Felicity into action. Rising, she walked out the back door, slipping her hands around her arms against the fall chill.

A stout man in a denim jacket was climbing down off the roof.

"What's wrong?" she asked.

"A new roof would solve your problems," he said heartily.

She made a decision. "Thank you. If I decide to do that, I'll call you."

His grin faded. "You don't have much choice since you're getting water inside the house. You know how it rains here in the fall. Better do something now."

"Thank you," she repeated. "I'll let you know."

He looked annoyed. "I'm going to be pretty busy next week. You're lucky I have a few days free this week."

"I'll let you know," she repeated firmly.

After he left, she stood looking up at the roof. The porch was only one story up. That wasn't so high. At least she could climb up and see if there were leaves in the gutters.

Moving with firm purpose, she went upstairs and changed into form-fitting jeans and a Vassar sweatshirt. Then, wearing the flowered cotton gloves she used when she repotted houseplants, she went out to the garage. It was a detached building behind the house that had once been a carriage house. A winding brick drive led down to it. She got the stepladder from it.

She knew she could ask Clark to help her, but something inside resisted that. This was *her* house and her responsibility. He had already done plumbing free of charge. Besides, how complicated could it be to scoop a few leaves out of a gutter?

As she dragged the ladder after her across the wet yard, leaving twin furrows in the grass, she admitted there was something else stopping her. She didn't feel easy enough with Clark to ask for favors. They were cordial with each other, and he listened intently when she explained about social situations, but she knew she'd enforced a definite reserve between them. He rarely smiled at her, and at times the air of formality between them was becoming a strain.

When she reached the house, it took all her energy to heave the ladder up against the side of the building. Breathless, she put her foot on the first rung, then the second.

When she reached the eighth step, her waist was at the level of the porch roof. Clark had been right. The gutters were full of wet leaves. Reaching in, she pulled out a handful. Below the fresh leaves lay slimy, decomposing ones.

"Yuck," she muttered.

She flung the leaves to the ground and forced herself to dip her hand in again. Disheartened, she looked at the long length of gutter still to be cleaned. Well, it had to be done. Gritting her teeth, she set to work. On the third handful, a worm dangled from her fingers. Even with gloves on, it was a nauseating feeling to see it wriggling. She flung it quickly aside.

Felicity tried to make the task more palatable by distracting herself with reciting pieces of poetry. She had finished "The Road Not Taken" and was trying to remember the fifth line of Hamlet's soliloquy when she leaned to the right to rake out another handful.

Suddenly, the ladder began to sway. She grabbed for support, but her hand caught only the flimsy gutter. It would never hold her, she knew, as the ladder listed further to the side.

She screamed as her feet slid to one side of the rung and the ladder lurched downward. Closing her eyes, she braced herself for the fall.

It never came.

Instead, the ladder righted itself. From below, she heard an angry male voice.

"What the hell are you doing?"

Shaking, she looked down to see Clark standing on the ground, his hands gripping the aluminum sides of the ladder.

"I—I was..." She sucked in a deep breath of air.

"Get down from there!"

She descended on wobbly knees.

His face was dark with wrath. "Don't you have any sense? You have to put the damned thing on solid footing or it won't hold."

"Please, don't shout at me." The fact she was frightened added hauteur to her words.

"I'm trying to keep you from getting your fool neck broken." He stalked off without another word.

Clark returned to his room fighting back anger. Damned little snob. If he hadn't caught her, she'd be nursing a broken arm right now. Or worse. But her reaction had been to tell him not to shout at her! Of course he had yelled. Who wouldn't? He had been scared when he came around the side of the house and saw the ladder about to fall.

Felicity was supposed to be teaching *him* manners, yet she hadn't expressed one word of gratitude. Of course, he thought with a bitter smile, he was only an ex-con who would be out of her life in less than two weeks.

He wondered if she was counting the days.

Pushing aside the art books that he had been leafing through before he'd heard something scraping along the roof and had gone to investigate, he threw himself down on the bed and lay with his hands clasped behind his neck.

Was it hard on her to be with an uncouth man like himself? It must be, for she was always distant, only offering instructions in a brisk voice.

He didn't mind keeping things impersonal. He spent far too much time watching her anyway. He noticed her lithe, elegant body and the classical lines of her face more than was healthy. She made him doubly aware he had not been with a woman in a very long time. Not only had he been out of the game for a while, but with Felicity, he was out of his league.

His body tensed as he recalled all the nights in prison he had yearned for someone soft and loving to curl up next to him. Okay, so he had wanted pure physical satisfaction part of the time. But other times he had ached for another person to hold him tenderly and care for him.

Not that he was thinking of Felicity Simmons in those terms. She was far too aloof to ever display the physical warmth he craved. Both of them would be better off when he was gone.

Abandoning the ladder at the side of the house, Felicity left the gutters uncleaned. Before it rained again, she would have to deal with the problem, but at the moment, she didn't want to face it.

The more she thought about Clark's scolding, the madder she got. People simply did not speak to her that way. And he, of all people, should not have. *He* was the one who suggested she do the work herself.

That evening, when Clark came down for dinner, she greeted him with cool hauteur. She had asked him to dress in suits and sport coats, the sort of clothes he would wear when he went to nice restaurants.

He sat down wearing what was evidently the nicest outfit he had, a navy serge that showed definite signs of age. The cuffs were fraying and the fabric was wearing on the elbows. Even in aging clothes, however, he looked more attractive than a lot of men she knew dressed in the best that money could buy. Curbing those thoughts, she forced herself back to the matter at hand.

"Tonight we're having asparagus tips," she said shortly. "And fresh crab. That tiny fork is to dig the crab out of the shell."

He nodded.

The friction hanging in the air was palpable. She knew the incident with the ladder was as much on his mind as it was on hers. Since they were going to be living under the same roof for several more days, it would be best to clear the air.

"I don't usually demand apologies," she began, "but since I am teaching you etiquette, I feel obliged to point out that your behavior this afternoon was inexcusable."

His eyes turned flinty. "You've got a nerve when you consider I saved your butt."

She reddened. "This is hardly the proper way to conduct a—"

"Let's throw away the kid gloves for a minute." He pointed the crab fork at her. "I came around the house and saw you about to bite the ground from ten feet up. I barely reached the ladder in time. Sure, I yelled at you. I was scared."

Scared? He had been afraid of something bad happening to her?

As she paused to examine that thought, he continued, "I guess where you come from, people don't get too excited about anything. Well, I'm sorry, but my emotions show through from time to time."

Guiltily, she cleared her throat and looked into eyes snapping with belligerence. "I guess we misunderstood each other," she murmured.

"I'd say we did," he agreed curtly.

She picked up the crab dish and held it forward. "Would you care for more?"

He hesitated, seemed about to speak, then wordlessly accepted the bowl.

"Pretty tasty," he said after a minute.

"Thank you." She felt tense stomach muscles uncoil. She knew Clark's spare compliment was his way of smoothing things over between them.

The subject was dropped. During the rest of dinner, she talked about introductions and the correct things to say to people when in those situations. But her thoughts were elsewhere. She felt warmer toward him because he had felt concern for her.

After a dessert of black forest cake, she pushed back her chair. "I've drawn up a tentative schedule for your lessons. Tonight I'm going to teach you some ballroom dances."

He glanced around uncomfortably. "What for?"

She blinked, surprised that he would question the need. "Why everyone must know how to waltz and fox-trot. After all, you're going to be working for a big company. They'll have Christmas parties and other social functions. You have to know the basics."

He shook his head. "I only want you to teach me things that will make me fit in better. I don't have to be able to pass for Prince Charles."

Shrugging delicately she said, "If you don't think you can learn."

"It's not a question of being able to learn. It's a question of not wanting to."

She said nothing.

"Look, where I come from, there's a certain type of guy who dances, and I'm not that kind of guy."

So that was why he didn't want to learn. "That was the furthest thing from my mind. You're one of the most masculine men I've ever met. I don't think any woman would question your—" She halted, embarrassed at what she had blurted out.

He grinned. "Go on. I'm listening."

Felicity rose abruptly. Avoiding his gaze, she announced, "We'll begin the dancing lessons in the drawing room."

In the drawing room, she put on "The Blue Danube." "This is a waltz. One, two, three. One, two, three. Hear the beat? That's all there is to it." She was self-conscious as she moved forward and held out her arms. Her words to him still rang vividly in her ears.

"What do I do?" he asked.

Taking a deep breath, she stepped in close, lifted his right arm to her waist and put his left out to the side, fitted into hers. Felicity tried to be calm and professional but other thoughts intruded. She knew he hadn't been this close to a woman for a long time. She felt the tension in his hand on her waist, and she saw the turmoil in his eyes when their gazes met.

"All you have to do is take a step forward, then to the right." An unaccustomed quiver overtook her voice as his hand tightened around her waist. She sensed he had forgotten their purpose was to dance. She had the distinct impression he had intended to pull her close against him. Then, remembering himself, he relaxed his hold and looked away.

Concentrate on the dancing, she told herself firmly. "One, two, three," she said and began to move with the music.

He followed with uneven steps. He was out of time, but Felicity kept dancing, giving him a chance to feel the rhythm and to relax. But when he moved the wrong way and his body brushed hard against hers, they both stiffened.

"Sorry," he muttered.

"Don't be so tense. It will come." But she was uptight, too, unable to concentrate on the strains of the music because of her awareness of his large hand enveloping her small one and the nearness of his taut body.

She kept her eyes trained firmly over his left shoulder as she continued to instruct him. "Smaller steps. That's it. And a little slówer."

"I feel stupid."

"You're doing fine."

Felicity glanced up then and saw him looking down at her with a smile at the edge of his mouth and a faint light twinkling in his eyes. "Have you taught other men to dance?" he asked.

"You're the first."

"I like being the first."

Her gaze fell away. She didn't think he had intended a double entendre, but she was aware of other "firsts" with men. She wondered if he assumed that she had a lot of bedroom experience. He would be wrong.

The record ended. Felicity slipped quickly out of his arms and went to make another selection. "How about another Strauss waltz?" She was talking for the sake of talking because the silence between them unnerved her.

"Fine by me."

As "Tales from the Vienna Woods" began, she moved back into his arms. This time he put his hand around her waist with more confidence. And he followed the music admirably.

"You're doing very well. You have a natural grace."

He chuckled dryly. "The guys back in prison would be glad to hear that."

She went tense.

"It bothers you for me to mention prison, doesn't it? Well, I did spend three years of my life there," he said flatly.

Felicity remained rigid. "I think you should refrain from bringing the subject up with people you meet in Boston. Some people might form bad judgments because of it."

"But not you?"

She glanced up at his hard, sardonic smile. She didn't answer. What would he think if he knew that his raw virility was far more troubling to her than the fact he had been in prison?

# Four

Clark arose the next morning feeling restless. The first few days after his release from prison, he had reveled in his freedom. In prison, he had worked in the machine shop during the day and spent his spare hours studying. He hadn't had much extra time. After the initial euphoria of being able to do whatever he wished whenever he wished, time was beginning to hang on his hands.

It would have been easier if he owned a car and didn't have to depend on the daily bus. Since he would need a car when he moved to Boston, now was as good a time as any to buy one, he decided. The problem was how to look for a car when he didn't have the means of getting around.

Reluctantly, he sought Felicity out in the library. She was sitting at a desk in front of the window. Her hair hung loose. He wondered if she had any idea how much he longed to touch her hair or that he thought it looked like silken strands that had been dipped in amber honey. The tips brushed against her shoulders where her oversize sweatshirt had slipped to one side. The view of her smooth, alabaster skin momentarily distracted him. Then he realized she was waiting for him to speak, watching him with wide, curious blue eyes.

"Are you busy?" he asked.

"I'm working on a new brochure about the bed and breakfast. Why?"

Hesitating, he slipped a hand into his jeans pocket. He had always hated asking for favors. It was particularly hard to ask something of the woman sitting with such dainty command at the writing desk.

She tilted her head to one side and her hair swept even further across her bare skin. His pushed his hands into his pockets, forcing aside the impulse to touch her flawless skin.

"Yes?"

He felt like a peasant making a request of royalty. "I need to buy a car. I wondered if you could take me to look for one."

"Yes, I could. In fact, I can do it now."

As she laid her pen aside, he had the impression she was glad for a distraction.

Minutes later they drove off in her car. Felicity drove while he carried a newspaper folded back to the used-car section.

"What sort of car are you looking for?" she asked conversationally.

"A cheap one."

"What color?"

He slanted a sideways look at her. Was she kidding? What difference did it make as long as it wasn't rusted too badly? "I don't much care."

"I like green," she commented.

The color of money, he thought, and was immediately annoyed with himself. She was helping him out, the least he could do was be appreciative. "Yeah, that's a nice color."

It was one of those Indian summer days of blue and gold. The leaves were beginning to fall even from the stubborn oaks. As she steered the car down the two-lane road, Felicity was glad for the opportunity to be outside. Work hadn't been going well on the brochure anyway. These days it was hard to concentrate on anything. She seemed constantly distracted, listening for footsteps.

She drove into the town of Wellfleet, where they looked at the first car. It was a 1976 model in nice shape, but the seller wanted more than Clark was willing to pay. No one was home at the second stop. The third try was at a small used-car lot that boasted no more than a dozen cars.

Felicity got out of her expensive import and looked around with dismay. Surely Clark wasn't going to buy one of these battered, rusting heaps.

But he was walking down the row of cars with his hands in his back pockets, inspecting them with more than casual interest.

The owner appeared, grinning and buttoning his coat as he crossed the lot from the small office. "What can I do you for?" he asked.

"Just looking," Clark said laconically.

"You came to the right place for that! Yes, sir. I'm Jed Waverly, and I can make you a good deal on anything you like."

Felicity ventured over to join the men at a dark blue car.

"This is a nice car," the salesman said. "Needs just a little work. I'll start it up if you'd like to pop the hood."

Clark opened the hood. Felicity stood alongside him and stared down at the engine. To her it was a maze of hoses and belts and gadgets.

"It's noisy," she said.

Jed Waverly returned. "What do you think?"

"Idles rough," Clark replied. "It's got a burned exhaust valve, doesn't it?"

"Yeah, it does," the salesman admitted.

Felicity shot Clark a surprised glance, impressed that he could tell so much so quickly. She was certain Stewart could not have, regardless of how well he might understand Verdi's *Rigoletto*.

"It would take a lot of work to fix it up," Clark continued. "I'd have to take the head off, have the valves ground, put on a new head gasket and probably a new manifold gasket."

Felicity turned to go. Naturally, Clark wasn't going to buy a car with all those problems. Who would?

But Jed Waverly was undaunted. "Yeah, it needs a little work, but I can make you a good deal."

"How much?"

Startled, she watched as the two men negotiated a price. The salesman agreed to bring the car to the inn the next day along with the papers. The two men parted with a handshake.

On the way home, as she guided her sleek car around a curve, she ignored her rule of not interfering in other people's affairs. "Why did you buy a car that needs so many repairs?"

"Because I couldn't afford one in good running order."

One look at the tight set of his jaw, and she knew she had hit a nerve. "I'm sorry. I didn't mean to offend you."

He shrugged brusquely. "Forget it."

The silence between them was strained during the rest of the drive. It was not until she stopped in front of the house that he spoke again, and then she could tell he was having to pull each word out.

"I hate to ask this, but do you think I could use your garage to work on the car once I get it?"

"Of course," she said quickly, anxious to make amends for having hurt his pride.

"Thank you." He got out and walked away without another word.

Sighing, she followed. At times she felt she and Clark might become friends. Then the barriers always snapped back into place. As a rule, she was more comfortable in keeping people at a distance than with being close. But the wall of reserve between her and Clark was beginning to disturb her more and more.

Two days later, Clark took the bus to Boston to find a place to rent.

He started by visiting his mother. He had gone to see her as soon as he was released from prison. She was sitting in almost the same spot in a well-lit room of the institution. Her shoulders were hunched forward in a way that made her look frail and defeated. After a brief, vague smile upon first seeing him, she sank back into gloom.

Clark stayed for almost an hour. He read her his latest letter from Larry. He talked about his new job and about coming to Boston to look for a place to live. He reminisced about old times when they were a family. Sometimes she showed momentary interest, but more often she sat slumped and impassive.

Discouraged, he finally rose. Bending to kiss her cheek, he promised, "I'll come to see you again soon."

He walked out of the building into the blustery cold feeling depressed and in need of someone to talk to. But he had no one. Aside from a brother and friends in prison, he was alone in the world. He felt that keenly as he set about the task of looking for an apartment to rent.

The entire time behind bars, he had dreamed of his own place. He wanted one with lots of windows so he could look out at the birds soaring and dipping and feel their freedom. He was willing to pay a lot for that luxury. He had been forced to economize on the car because he didn't have much money at the moment. But once he started working, he could afford to rent a nice place, and he did have enough cash for a down payment.

Turning up the collar of his coat, he stopped at a newsstand and bought a paper. As the wind blew past him, he took a pen from the pocket of his old wool coat and circled five apartments that appealed to him.

He rode the bus to the first one. It was in a nice new building with a view of the water. He pushed through shiny brass doors and paused to look with respect at the mauve-colored walls. The rent was high but not more than he could afford once he started his job.

But the crisp landlord didn't rent to just anyone. He wanted references, and he wanted to know where Clark had been living. Clark wasn't going to lie.

Once the landlord learned of his record, the interview was over.

He had the same problem at the next stop, where an elegant older woman with long pink fingernails confided she didn't think he would be happy there.

His third attempt was with a jovial Italian man who shook his head, still grinning. "Don't think I'd want to rent to you. Sorry. Best of luck somewhere else."

It was a humiliating experience.

Clark ended up looking at a shabbily furnished efficiency in a decaying building not far from the docks. Rusty pipes were exposed and a noisy radiator clanked the whole time a plump, gum-chewing woman showed him the room. It was the kind of place that accepted men with pasts like his.

For a moment, he felt a whiplash of anger at Larry for putting him in this situation, then he pushed that aside. He could go through his whole life being bitter and it wouldn't change anything, he reflected as his old resignation settled back over him.

"I'll take it," he said tonelessly. The wire mesh on the ground-floor window was meant to keep people from breaking it, but it was a depressing reminder of the iron bars he had looked through for the past three years.

Later, walking around the city, he brooded on how much his life was affected by his record. He had been lucky to get the job with the computer company. There, too, he knew he would be watched closely.

Today's attempt at renting a place had made him painfully aware how different he was from other men. Whether he had actually committed the crime was beside the point; he was marked for life as someone not to be trusted. Was he wasting time and money to learn social skills? After all, nothing could change the fact that he had a criminal record.

And what kind of social life could he have once he moved to Boston? He liked women, but he wondered what it would be like to be intimate with one again. It had been long enough for him to feel nervous, almost like it would be his first time.

The only female who had shown any interest in him at all was the younger sister of a fellow inmate. Lauren had sent him a few letters and come to visit a time or two. He hadn't heard from her in the past year, but he knew she lived in Boston.

He was lonely and enough in need of a friendly word to stop at a phone booth and call her.

Lauren was surprised but pleased to hear from him. "How are you?" she asked warmly.

"Fine. I came into town to find a place to live. I'm going to start a job here shortly."

"Listen, you caught me at a bad time. I was just on my way out the door, but if you're going to be back in Boston, we'll have to get together," she said brightly.

"I'd like that." He hesitated, then asked, "How about this Friday night?"

* * *

Felicity spent the day Clark was in Boston giving piano lessons, writing letters and organizing the pantry shelves. It was the time of year when night encroaches further and further into the daytime, and by five o'clock darkness had fallen.

She had not realized how much she was waiting for the sound of the front door until she heard footsteps in the hallway.

Quickly, she pushed the last can of carrots into the pantry and started into the hall, pulling her red turtleneck down over close-fitting black corduroy slacks as she went.

Clark was hanging his worn wool coat in the closet when she entered the foyer.

"Hello," she greeted him. "Did you find an apartment?"

"Yes."

He sounded tired and unhappy. Had something bad happened in Boston? She wanted to ask but hesitated. Gram Simmons had always said if someone wanted something known, he would tell it. Otherwise, it was rude to pry. Still, Clark looked so dejected that she wanted to offer some comfort.

Before she had a chance to speak, he said, "I think I'll go upstairs and take a shower before dinner." Turning, he ascended the stairs.

She stood alone in the entryway. What was he thinking? Or feeling? There was so much she didn't know about Clark Fielding. Before, it hadn't mattered so much. But more and more she found herself wanting to understand him better.

Later, as they sat across from each other in the elegant dining room over a dinner of *boeuf bourguignon*, she asked, "What is the name of the firm where you'll be working?"

"The Electric Abacus. It's a computer company."

She nodded, encouraging him to continue talking. Maybe it would put him in a better mood and take his mind off whatever was bothering him. "What will you do there?"

"I'll write programs for business."

"Did you have that kind of a job before you, well," she hesitated, "before you went to prison?"

The question didn't seem to offend him. "No, I took courses while I was inside. Before, I'd done construction work."

No wonder he had such broad, well-developed shoulders, she thought. She waited, hoping he would continue.

"Working in an office, wearing suits, acting polite, all that will be new to me. Those aren't the kind of people I'm used to." He flashed a brief grin. "But I might as well get my feet wet by putting some of what I've learned into practice. I was thinking of a play and dinner in a nice restaurant in Boston. Does that sound appropriate?"

A smile overcame Felicity. It had been a while since she had been to Boston, and she longed to see live theater again. At the back of her mind, even though she didn't take it out and examine it, was the thought it would be nice to spend an evening out with Clark. "When?" she asked.

"Friday night."

Felicity reviewed possible outfits. Her black wool looked chic and classy with her black boots, but she was inclined to wear something softer and more feminine. Perhaps her yellow, shoulderless dress.

"That sounds fine," she said. "We'll check the paper to see what plays are showing."

"Do you think it's better to have dinner before or after the play?"

"A late-night dinner can be very elegant." Smiling, she confessed, "I get too hungry. I always like to eat before the play."

"I imagine Lauren will like that, too."

Felicity sat motionless. Clark was not asking her to dinner and a play. He was taking someone else.

"Maybe a drink afterward?" he asked.

"Yes, that would be tasteful." Her words were formal and stilted. She felt foolish for having presumed he meant to invite her. And hurt that he did not want to go with her.

Rising abruptly, she said, "If you'll excuse me, I'm going to my room to read."

"Before you go, I wondered if... That is—" He glanced down at his clothes. "I'm going to have to have something to wear. I need to buy some new clothes for my job anyway. But I don't have any idea what's in style. I was hoping you could help me pick out some things."

He was asking for her help, she thought with an empty feeling in her stomach. Well, that was what he was paying her for, wasn't it? "I can assist you in making selections," she said tersely.

"I appreciate it," he said sincerely. "Could we go tomorrow afternoon?"

"That sounds fine." She swept out of the room without a backward glance, her regal exit concealing her unhappiness. Once in her room, however, her head was not so high. She paced to the window, twitched back the curtain and stared forlornly out into the darkness.

So Clark had a date with another woman? He had every right. And she had no right to feel—what did she feel? If she hadn't known better, she might have identified it as jealousy.

But that would have implied she and Clark had a more personal relationship than actually existed. When all was said and done, he was only a man who was renting a room from her.


Gram Simmons's visit was completely unexpected. She arrived the next day by cab, her iron-gray curls lacquered into place and her jaw set in a tense line.

"I shall never," she informed Felicity as she sailed into the house, "do that again. The man was completely insane. He drove like a maniac."

Felicity nodded gravely and translated that to mean the driver had pushed the speedometer above fifty miles an hour. It would have been so much simpler for Gram to hire a chauffeur, but she was too proud to admit that her deteriorating vision and shaky hands made driving a permanent impossibility. Instead, she kept her top-of-the-line Mercedes in the four-car garage behind her Beacon Hill home and took cabs, emerging each time with the declaration she would not be caught dead in one again.

Felicity led her grandmother upstairs to an airy corner bedroom where Gram looked around critically. "I hope this room won't be drafty."

"Would you rather be in the red room down the hall?"

"No, it's too poorly ventilated. And the room with the brass bed gets too much light in the morning." She moved around the room, running her hand over the top of the empire chest and then unabashedly checking her fingertips for dust.

"There's someone in the blue room anyway." Felicity had seen Clark going out to the garage this morning to work on his car. She had left him food in warm chafing dishes for breakfast and then gone into town to buy groceries. Although she wouldn't have admitted it aloud, she was avoiding him. It was easier not to have to look into those clear gray eyes and try to analyze why she felt so disappointed about him taking another woman out.

In an effort to change the direction of her thoughts, she opened Gram's suitcase and began removing the clothes her grandmother's maid had carefully folded.

The old woman subsided into a burgundy high-backed wing chair. "Have you given any more thought to coming back to Boston?"

Felicity smiled over her shoulder. "You know the answer to that."

Gram exhaled a long-suffering sigh. "It never hurts to ask. Sooner or later you're bound to see reason."

"I like it here. You know that."

"Oh, I admit the Cape is very well in its place," she conceded loftily. "Your grandfather and I used to enjoy the odd weekend here. But, really, dear, one can overdo quaintness. Being in Boston keeps one so much more levelheaded."

Felicity chuckled. "Have I told you yet that I'm glad you came?" She reinforced her words with a quick peck on her grandmother's withered cheek.

As a child, she had longed for the hugs from her grandmother that she had received so lavishly from her parents. But all Gram ever gave were light kisses on the cheek. Felicity had come to realize that didn't mean Gram loved her less, only that she had difficulty expressing her affection. Sometimes, Felicity wondered about her own capacity for showing warmth. After a lifetime of having reserve drilled into her, she didn't open up easily to people.

Gram patted her hand and conceded, "You're a good child."

"Come downstairs, and I'll make tea. I have some lovely shortbread to go with it. We're not completely uncivilized here, you know," she added with a teasing smile.

"I never said you were. Still, there are so many *essentials* that aren't available."

"We do have grocery stores," Felicity noted as they headed down to the kitchen.

Her grandmother pursed her lips. "I am speaking of the opera and chamber concerts and well you know it."

Felicity missed her chance to reply when the back door opened and Clark stepped in. His cheeks were ruddy from the breeze, his dark hair was wind-tossed, and he was wearing a faded, torn jacket. His hands were black with grease and grime.

Gram stared.

"Th—this is Clark Fielding," Felicity stammered. It wasn't often that she felt awkward, but this was one of those moments. "He's staying here. Clark, this is my grandmother, Mrs. Simmons."

Gram was at her most formidable. "How do you do, Mr. Fielding?" Her already strong Brahman accent seemed to gain strength.

"Fine, thanks." He looked at his hands. "Nice meetin' you." Nodding uncomfortably, he slipped out of the room.

"Do your guests generally use the kitchen entrance?" Gram demanded.

"He is not an ordinary guest. He's here on a longer-term basis." Felicity didn't want to explain further, but she could sense her grandmother's sharpened interest.

"Indeed?" The old woman's hard gaze remained on her as she put water on to boil. "Precisely how long has this young man been here?"

"A few days."

"And how long does he mean to stay?"

"A few more days," she said vaguely and tried for a change of subject. "How are things with the bridge club?"

"Those women are impossible. But that is quite beside the point. You are acting in a most peculiar and evasive manner."

"I am not," Felicity denied emphatically.

"Of course you are. I could always tell, even when you were a little girl, when you didn't want me to know something. Is there something particular about Mr. Fielding that you wish to hide?" Her grandmother folded her hands across the matronly bosom of her wine-red knit dress.

"Of course not."

Gram was silent until Felicity had carried the tea into the parlor. When they were seated across a silver tea service from each other, she took up the attack again. "Where is Mr. Fielding from?"

"Boston."

The faded eyes registered interest. "Is he related to the Hargrove Fieldings who own the Plaza Federal Bank?"

"I think it unlikely." Listen to me, Felicity thought in exasperation. I've been with Gram for half an hour and already I'm talking like her. She rephrased the sentence, "I don't think so."

"To whom is he related?"

"I'm not sure he still has relatives in Boston." She busied herself spooning sugar into her tea. As a rule, she was honest with her grandmother, but she felt an unexplained need to protect Clark from Gram's disapproval.

"Where does he live?"

"He doesn't have a permanent address yet. Actually, he has been living away from Boston for the past few years." She bit into a shortbread to forestall further questions. It was a hopeless tactic. Gram pursued.

"Where has he been residing?"

Felicity thought of half a dozen lies. She could have said she didn't know. But that smacked of being ashamed of Clark. Besides, lies usually bred more lies. The truth was the best course. "Prison."

Her grandmother fixed her with an unrelenting stare. "Let me understand this perfectly..."

That was always Gram's lead-in to something she already understood very well. "The man has a criminal record and you are living here, quite alone and unprotected, with him." Faded blue eyes snapped.

"Have you taken complete and total leave of your senses, child?"

"He isn't dangerous." At least not in ways her grandmother might think, Felicity thought fleetingly. But there was danger in the sideways glances he sometimes threw at her and in his slow, sensual smiles and in the dimple that formed a tantalizing dent in his left cheek.

"Humph. I suggest that you are not qualified to make that determination. Which is another reason you should live in Boston, like any reasonable young woman, instead of at the edge of nowhere."

Felicity tried to circumvent an argument by pointing out, "Your tea is getting cold."

Her grandmother vigorously stirred in a spoonful of sugar, but she was not to be deterred. "You may not have any concern for your own safety, but I do."

"Gram, I'm perfectly all right living here. No one is going to harm me." She glanced furtively over her shoulder, praying that Clark was not within hearing distance.

After a further moment of clinking the spoon around the teacup, her grandmother grudgingly admitted, "I daresay if the man intended harm, he would have already done so. Perhaps you are safe. Thank the Lord you have more sense than to develop an interest in a man of his caliber. Some women actually find that outlaw sort attractive. Can you imagine?"

Felicity wordlessly ate another piece of short-bread.

"Stewart asked about you the other day," her grandmother continued.

"How is he?" She was glad for the change of subject.

"As dashing as ever. I remain constantly surprised that some woman hasn't snapped him up by now."

"Oh, Gram, women have careers these days. They don't think solely in terms of marriage."

"Don't deceive yourself. When all is said and done, having a family is what counts."

As Felicity carried the tea service back to the kitchen, she reviewed those words and recalled the love and security she had felt with her parents. What would it be like to belong to someone wholly again? To be cherished and cuddled and ache to be with that person? She couldn't answer those questions. She only knew she felt a sense of profound emptiness.

# Five

Clark found the weathered clapboard garage a cold place to work. The wind blowing in off the water seeped through the loose windowpanes and added to the chill. It would have been nicer to work on his car in a heated garage, but he had never had the luxury before so he supposed he shouldn't expect it now.

He remembered the time he had helped Larry work on his first car. They had put a transmission in the old Ford, working out on the street in front of their run-down tenement building. Larry had been good with cars—when he took the time to concentrate instead of thinking about the next way he could get rich quick.

At least prison seemed to have made Larry more mature and responsible. The tone of his infrequent letters had changed over the past three years. Now he talked about his hopes of finding a job as a mechanic when he got out instead of dreaming about new schemes to chase the rainbow to its pot of gold.

As Clark slid under the car and lay on his back on the chilly concrete floor, he thought about Felicity and how different their lives had been. If he'd had any doubts about the advantages to which she was accustomed, the arrival of her grandmother had shattered them.

Dinner last night had been tough. He had taken his seat in his usual place, only to realize the old woman was still standing, glaring at him as if he'd just crawled out from under a rock.

"It's proper to pull a chair out for a lady," Felicity had murmured.

Feeling foolish and awkward, he rose and held the chair for Mrs. Simmons. She sniffed her thanks, then proceeded to establish beyond all doubt that he was not in their set. She talked about friends at the country club, then about a lavish charity ball she wanted Felicity to attend and that some guy named Stewart would be going to. Felicity had mostly sat quietly. A time or two, he had seen her stealing glances at him. That had only made him more ill at ease. He wondered if she was comparing him to the men who would be at the charity ball. He knew he would come out the loser in such a comparison.

Reaching for a wrench, he tightened a bolt, then crawled out from under the car.

As he wiped the grease from his hands, he reflected that Felicity would someday be a rich woman. In spite of the sometimes vulnerable expressions he saw on her face, there was no need to worry about her. She would be well taken care of.

So when he went into the house ten minutes later, he shouldn't have cared that the doorknob was loose on the back door. Yet he found himself going down into the basement, searching at the tool bench for a screwdriver and tightening the set screw.

Felicity arrived as he was finishing the task. A cheerful blue apron with flour speckled across it was tied around her slender waist.

"Thank you," she said. "I've been meaning to call someone about that. I was afraid the doorknob was going to fall off."

He sighed. "You don't have to call anyone for something this simple." How could she know so much about manners and so little about practical things? It was clear that repairmen took advantage of her. The least he could do was prevent her from calling one when the job was small.

"I wasn't going to get a repairman just for one thing," she defended herself. "There are several odd jobs around here to be done."

"Like what?" She looked pretty today, he noted, with her hair swinging loose around her face. The dab of flour on her aristocratic nose made her look comical and that warmed him toward her.

"Well, one of the burners on the stove isn't working."

"I'll take care of it."

She hesitated before saying reluctantly, "I can't ask you to do that."

He smiled, amused because she so obviously wished him to override her objections. "If you had the money to pay for it, the jobs would already have been done. Right?"

"That's true," she admitted.

"Since you don't have the money, you might as well let me do it."

A frown gathered on her brow. "But I feel I'm taking advantage of you."

"Let me worry about that." She looked mussed and domestic in her apron. And sexy. Although he was constantly aware of her graceful curves, he was not always so aware of her sensuality.

Or maybe he deliberately ignored that part of her because he had been away from women for so long he didn't know how to deal with his feelings. Or his desires. So it was best to keep himself out of range.

Briskly, he picked up the screwdriver and headed out the door. If he didn't leave, he thought, he'd try to take that smudge of flour off her nose. Or run his hands over her hips. What would Grandma think if she came in and found the village derelict dallying with her high-born granddaughter?

What would Felicity think?

Clark would have been surprised to know that Felicity might not have objected. Even though he was wearing a torn jacket and his hair was askew, he looked ruggedly appealing. That made it even harder for her to think of him Friday evening with another woman.

The torn jacket reminded her how much he needed new clothes, and that reminded her she had promised to go shopping with him.

Guiltily, she said, "Clark, wait."

He turned back. "I'm afraid I forgot we had plans to go shopping yesterday. Anyway, this is Tuesday, and I know you need something new before Friday night." She hurried past that, not wanting to think about his date. "I'm going into town in a few minutes. You could go along if you like, and we could shop."

Gram had announced her intention of taking a nap and had disappeared up the stairs half an hour ago, so it seemed safe to sneak out with him. Last night Felicity had been painfully aware her grandmother disliked Clark, and she had no desire to bring the two together any more than necessary. It was uncomfortable for everyone.

He shrugged. "I guess we could do that. Give me a minute to change."

By the time he arrived back downstairs, however, Felicity heard Gram coming to the head of the stairway. Glancing up, she saw that her grandmother was wearing a severe gray dress and a no-nonsense felt hat. Gram never ventured out in public without a hat.

"Are you going with us?" Felicity asked, trying to conceal her dismay.

"Yes, I believe I will. A good breath of air is always good for the constitution."

Under her breath, Felicity murmured, "Oh, dear." Aloud, she said, "Clark is going, too. He needs to buy some clothes, and that might take a while. You're welcome to go, but you might be bored."

"I know how long shopping can take," Gram said frostily. "I used to go with your grandfather to his tailor's. Since I have no other pressing business to attend to, I might as well ride along."

Felicity knew Gram's stubborn nature well enough to realize nothing would dissuade her now that her mind was made up. Besides, Felicity had not missed the old woman's sharp, suspicious glance at Clark. It said plainly she did not want her granddaughter alone with this man. Felicity was convinced Clark had not missed that look. His lips were pressed into a grim, brooding line.

It was going to be a long day, she thought unhappily. "Well, we might as well get started."

Gram marched outside and got into the passenger's seat of the elegant car. Clark got in back. Felicity slid in the driver's seat and started the engine. In a moment, they were on the road.

"Not too fast, dear."

"Yes, Gram."

Felicity steered carefully around a broad curve.

"Watch that truck up ahead."

"I am."

"Don't get too close to the center."

"I won't."

It went on like that. During the next five minutes, Gram cautioned her at every step. It was beginning to get to Felicity.

"Be careful you don't go off onto the shoulder here."

"She's fine," Clark put in from the back seat.

"I was merely helping her—"

"Well, don't. You're making her nervous by harping at her."

Felicity tensed. Of all the things *not* to say to her grandmother.

Gram's chin went up militantly. "Young man, I think I know a good deal more about driving than you. I was behind the wheel before you were born. I might add I was never once in a major accident."

"I'll bet you caused a few, though."

Felicity cringed. The tension was thick enough to cut with a knife.

"Mr. Fielding, for your information—"

Clark interrupted again. "Look at the way traffic is backed up behind us. People are weaving all over trying to find a place to pass. She needs to go faster, not slower."

"Apparently," Gram said in a voice thick with disapproval, "you are not aware that speed kills."

Felicity's knuckles were white from gripping the wheel. She pulled off the road in front of a steepled country church. As a string of cars rushed by, she put a hand to her forehead. "Please, both of you. You're driving me crazy. Just sit there and be quiet!"

She couldn't remember the last time she had raised her voice at anyone. It simply was not done. Most specifically, she could not believe she had shouted at her grandmother.

But she had. Gram sat stiff with shock. Felicity glanced into the back seat and saw a small smile touching the corners of Clark's mouth. His expression seemed to say, Good for you.

Flustered, she started the car again. During the rest of the drive, her passengers were silent. Gram sat puffed up like an affronted bantam, but for once Felicity ignored the silent disapproval. She glanced again into the rearview mirror and saw Clark looking almost cheerful.

For some strange reason, that calmed her. Reaching over, she patted her grandmother's hand and smiled gently. Gram relented enough to nod.

They reached Orson's Fine Men's Clothing, and Felicity parked in front of the gold and black striped awning. "We're here," she announced needlessly. She was grateful to escape from the car.

Clark got out and opened her grandmother's door. The three of them went into the store together. While

Clark walked toward the shirts, Gram pulled Felicity aside.

"Perhaps I was offering a bit too much advice," she said tautly. "But a driver does not always see everything, and two pairs of eyes are better than one."

"I understand."

The old woman cast a dark glance toward Clark. "That one certainly isn't timid about speaking his mind."

"No harm was done," Felicity soothed.

"That's a matter of opinion. In my day, young men did not speak to their elders so rudely."

Clark crossed to the sport coats and frowned at the selection. A dapper clerk with a carnation in his lapel was occupied with the store's only other customer. "I'd better go help Clark," Felicity said quickly.

It was a vain hope of escape. Gram followed, her head tilted up defiantly.

"Finding anything?" Felicity asked him.

He shook his head. "I don't really know what to look at."

She touched one of the coats. "This is an attractive suede jacket."

Her grandmother sniffed. "It won't go with anything. A Harris tweed is much better. Or this dark gray wool might look good on you," she conceded critically and thrust the jacket at Clark.

He accepted it tentatively. "I don't know. It looks a little—"

"Don't argue with me, young man. Try it on," she commanded.

It was the first time Felicity had seen Clark's meek side. The anger he had exhibited in the car was gone. Mutely, he slipped the coat on and stood for inspection.

Felicity noted with approval how well the charcoal gray brought out the powerful gray of his eyes.

Gram was not so appreciative. She circled him with a narrowed, fault-seeking gaze. "Not bad," she pronounced reluctantly. "With a pinstripe shirt and the right tie, I daresay you could pass muster."

Clark looked toward the array of ties. "Would that blue one be okay?"

"Don't be ridiculous. It's completely wrong. The blue one indeed!" Muttering her irritation, Gram searched the rack of ties. "Here, put this on. In fact, go into the dressing room and put on a pinstripe shirt and that light gray pair of trousers."

Clark hesitated.

"You should try them on to see how they look together." Felicity added a smile to soften her grandmother's curt words.

He almost smiled back at her. Did she imagine the ghost of humor touching his eyes briefly? Something in his gaze seemed to say, "I won't make this any harder for you, Felicity."

He turned and headed toward the dressing room; her grandmother went off in search of further possibilities.

Felicity did not know it could be so scintillating to watch a man emerge from the dressing room in different combinations of clothes. Ordinarily, she wouldn't have waited by a man's dressing room with such anticipation. But then most men didn't look so broad-shouldered, narrow-hipped and stoically handsome as Clark. His dark hair grew increasingly mussed from slipping in and out of shirts and jackets, but that only made him look more boyish and appealing.

By the time the salesclerk was free, he didn't dare interfere. Gram had released Clark from the dressing room but she still marched around the store with fierce purpose, narrowly examining the shirts and frowning over the slacks.

Clark stood by Felicity awkwardly holding an armload of clothes. "Do you really think these clothes are okay?" he worried.

"They're perfect. Gram has always had an excellent sense of fashion. And she goes to enough board meetings to know what the well-dressed young executive is wearing these days."

"Good."

"You realize we'll have to let her back-seat drive on the way home," she murmured.

A slow grin spread over his face. "Yeah, I guess we will."

Felicity didn't know if her shiver of pleasure was in response to his magical dimple and the warm glint in his eyes or the sense of friendship between them. All she knew was that she was in no hurry to move away and break the spell.

Finally, however, Gram sailed up, unloaded three shirts and two more ties into his hands and barked, "Buy these."

He did.

While Clark checked out his purchases, Gram confided to Felicity, "He's dreadfully stubborn, but he does wear clothes well."

Felicity felt warmed all over by those few words of praise by her grandmother.

"Pity he could never be trusted," Gram concluded and walked out the door.

Felicity's grandmother left for Boston the next day, climbing into a cab with the warning she did not expect to make it back alive.

That evening, Felicity made coq au vin for dinner. While she had a bottle of wine out for cooking, she decided to give Clark a lesson on wines. It was something he would need to know when dining in the finer restaurants.

Resolutely ignoring the fact he would be in one of those restaurants tomorrow night with another woman, she carried four bottles into the dining room and set them on the table.

Clark looked at them with mild interest.

"Do you know anything about wine?" she asked.

"I've drunk a few bottles in my time," he drawled.

"About the bouquet and decanting, I mean."

"No."

"Okay." She sat down. "I've brought both red and white wines. Naturally, with white meat like chicken, one would serve a white wine."

"Of course."

She glanced suspiciously at him. He looked perfectly serious, but she thought she detected amusement in his voice. Did he think she was acting pompous?

"We'll begin with a nice Cabernet Sauvignon," she said briskly. "At all the better restaurants, the man is given a sample before the glasses are filled. You are to taste it and indicate your approval."

She poured a small amount into a glass and passed it to him.

He drank it. "Tastes fine to me."

"Good. Now we'll try some of this domestic wine."

As they ate, she poured samples from each of the bottles on the table. All the while, she talked about vintage years and body. Felicity prided herself on her knowledge of wines, and she was giving Clark a thorough lecture. She hoped he was paying close attention.

He seemed to be. At least his eyes rarely strayed from her face.

Over the course of the meal, she had four—or was it five?—glasses. She was feeling relaxed and in a pleasant frame of mind by the time she pushed her plate aside. When she dropped her fork, she giggled.

"Clumsy me," she murmured. Why was he watching her with that curious smile? Oh! He thought she was tipsy. She laughed at the idea. Then it occurred to her she *was* tipsy, and she laughed even harder.

His grin deepened.

Cupping her chin in her hands, she looked across the table at him. "Do you know how sexy your smile is?"

He chuckled. "Funny, but the guys in the cell block never mentioned that."

"A lot they know." She tossed her head. It cleared momentarily, and she realized with a start that she was telling a man she found his smile sexy. Then the cozy haze settled over her again, and she was completely at ease, slipping her shoes off and letting her toes wriggle on the thick carpet.

"What do you like in a woman?" she asked, pushing her toes more firmly into the soft rug. This was blatant flirting and she knew it. But so what?

"I like a woman who can hold her liquor."

His eyes were bright with humor. Really, she noted, he was devastatingly handsome when he smiled.

# The more
# you love romance . . .
# the more
# you'll love this offer

# FREE!

*Mail this heart today! (See inside)!*

## Join us on a Silhouette® Honeymoon
## and we'll give you
## 4 free books
## A free manicure set
## And a free mystery gift

# IT'S A
# SILHOUETTE HONEYMOON —
# A SWEETHEART
# OF A FREE OFFER!

## HERE'S WHAT YOU GET:

### 1. Four New Silhouette Desire® Novels — FREE!

Take a Silhouette Honeymoon with your four exciting romances — yours FREE from Silhouette Books. Each of these hot-off-the-press novels brings you the passion and tenderness of today's greatest love stories . . . your free passports to bright new worlds of love and foreign adventure.

### 2. A compact manicure set — FREE!

You'll love your beautiful manicure set — an elegant and useful accessory to carry in your handbag. Its rich burgundy case is a perfect expression of your style and good taste — and it's yours free with this offer!

### 3. An Exciting Mystery Bonus — FREE!

You'll be thrilled with this surprise gift. It will be the source of many compliments, as well as a useful and attractive addition to your home.

### 4. Money-Saving Home Delivery!

Join the Silhouette Desire subscriber service and enjoy the convenience of previewing 6 new books every month delivered right to your home. Each book is yours for only $2.24 — 26¢ less per book than what you pay in stores. And there is no extra charge for postage and handling. Great savings plus total convenience add up to a sweetheart of a deal for you!

### 5. Free Newsletter!

You'll get our monthly newsletter, packed with news on your favorite writers, upcoming books, even recipes from your favorite authors.

### 6. More Surprise Gifts!

Because our home subscribers are our most valued readers, we'll be sending you additional free gifts from time to time — as a token of our appreciation.

**START YOUR SILHOUETTE HONEYMOON TODAY — JUST COMPLETE, DETACH AND MAIL YOUR FREE-OFFER CARD**

# Get your fabulous gifts
## ABSOLUTELY FREE!

**MAIL THIS CARD TODAY.**

## GIVE YOUR HEART TO SILHOUETTE

**Yes!** Please send me my four Silhouette Desire novels FREE, along with my free manicure set and free mystery gift as explained on the opposite page.

NAME _____
(PLEASE PRINT)

ADDRESS _____ APT. _____

CITY _____ STATE _____

ZIP CODE _____

225 CIY JAYA

Prices subject to change. Offer limited to one per household and not valid to present subscribers.

## SILHOUETTE BOOKS "NO-RISK" GUARANTEE

— There's no obligation to buy — and the free books and gifts remain yours to keep.

— You pay the lowest price possible and receive books before they appear in stores.

— You may end your subscription any time — just write and let us know.

PLACE HEART STICKER HERE

# START YOUR
# SILHOUETTE HONEYMOON TODAY.
# JUST COMPLETE, DETACH AND MAIL YOUR
# FREE-OFFER CARD.

If offer card below is missing, write to:
Silhouette Books, 901 Fuhrmann Blvd., P.O. Box 9013, Buffalo, N.Y. 14240-9013

"What else?" Leaning forward, she propped her elbows on the table.

"Someone sensitive. And smart. Being pretty helps," he added honestly.

"Is your date tomorrow night pretty?"

"I think so."

Felicity's mouth formed a pout. She didn't want him to go out with someone pretty. Why didn't he stay here with her where he belonged? That thought had not occurred to her before, but it seemed reasonable.

"I'll bet she doesn't know anything about wines," she noted meanly. Somewhere she heard a stern voice saying, "Felicity Simmons, what is wrong with you? You are making a fool of yourself." She ignored the voice.

"I'm sure she's not as knowledgeable as you," he agreed. His smile was coupled with a look of sensual speculation. His eyes skimmed over her face like a caress.

"I'll bet she doesn't know the difference between a Sparkling Saumur and a Sparkling Vouvray."

His laughter was low and husky. "At the moment, I wonder if you do either."

Her head came up proudly. "Of course I do. A Saumur is a white wine from the Loire. And a Vouvray has extra sugar added to give it bubbles." She frowned, then wondered aloud, "Or do I have that backward?"

"I don't know." His eyes remained on her, warm and filled with amusement.

"I'll check. I have a bottle of each." Felicity pushed her chair back from the table and started to rise. For some reason, her legs were not working properly, and she could not lift herself into a standing position. She tried again without success.

"Hmmm," she muttered, frowning her confusion.

Clark rose and came around the table to her. Circling her waist with strong hands, he pulled her to her feet.

"I don't un-erstand. I never have trouble standing." Her words sounded muffled, unclear.

"You're going to have even more trouble walking." Suddenly, he bent and swept her up into his arms. She probably should have resisted, but it was too much trouble. Instead, she closed her eyes, feeling the motion of his body as he walked and then a gentle swaying as he began mounting the steps. Moments later, he laid her atop the bed. She opened her eyes to find herself in her room. It was illuminated only by a light filtering in from the hall.

"I wasn't through telling you about wine," she objected in a small voice.

"Oh, yes, you were." His voice was rich with suppressed laughter.

She felt his fingers moving on her waist and realized he was loosening her green silk blouse. His big hands felt good on her body. She smiled and stretched lazily so that her whole body moved. "Going to tuck me in?"

There was a long hesitation, followed by a ragged sigh. "I was trying to make you more comfortable. If I had any sense, though, I'd leave this minute."

"Why?" Her words were a throaty blur.

"Because you look too tempting lying there with your cheeks flushed and your willpower down. I don't want to test my conscience." He straightened abruptly.

"Aren't you even going to give me a good-night kiss?" Through a haze, she saw him turn back to her and stand with his hands clenched into hard balls at his side. Why would he be tense? She stretched her arms upward in invitation.

That seemed to decide him.

"I must be crazy," he muttered. Then he was on the bed beside her, bending over her.

His first kiss grazed her cheek chastely, and she frowned. That was not what she wanted. Folding her hands around his neck, she touched his mouth with hers. He groaned heavily, then covered her lips with moist fervor.

With a whimper of approval, she snuggled closer. She was already warm from the wine, but now her body tingled with a greater heat. His kiss became more intense as he slipped the tip of his tongue between her teeth and stroked across her tongue. Breathlessly, she arched up toward him.

His arms formed a tight lock around her, and his mouth claimed hers with greater urgency. His tongue danced against hers, and his lips moved with hungry intensity. Her whole body was flushed, and she trembled with expectation. His kisses held promises and reservations all at the same time. Knowing he was trying to hold back and not succeeding made his caresses all the more tantalizing.

Her body, already softened from the effects of the wine, grew even more malleable. She complied readily when his hands slid below her waist, and he lifted her hips snugly against his. Their bodies fit together perfectly.

Letting her head tilt back, she opened her lips to invite a deeper kiss. As his tongue thrust in and out of her mouth, she stroked her fingers up and down his back in unconscious time to the rhythm. Her whole body felt tender, yearning, ripe for loving.

Suddenly, he broke free.

Lying beside him, she felt the thudding of his heart against her chest and his warm quick breaths against her cheek. But she didn't sense that he was withdrawing until he sat up. Without another word, he left the room, closing the door behind him.

He would be back, she thought with a blissful smile and curled up to wait. He would be back.

Clark didn't sleep at all that night. He lay on his bed, willing his tense body to relax. But all he could think about was the woman down the hall. It would have been so easy to have taken her. And so wrong.

At the moment, his body hated his scruples. How many times had he heard men in the cell block describe in crude and graphic detail what they would do with a woman as soon as they were out? He had not been without his own desires and fantasies during that endless, three-year stretch.

Yet he could not take advantage of her. It would be a sacrilege for a man like him to make love to a woman like Felicity under any circumstances, but especially when she had had too much to drink.

There were, he admitted, other things holding him back. He wasn't sure he could trust himself to be gentle. It had been so long that raw passion might overcome all else. What if he hurt her? It was best to stay here in his room where nothing could happen.

He only hoped Felicity would not remember the night's events when she awoke in the morning.

# Six

Felicity blinked and felt an uncomfortable pounding in her head. The sun spreading a blanket of gold over her floor affirmed that it was morning. Time to get up. But when she threw back the cover and sat up, the pounding in her head turned into a roar. She slumped back onto the pillow.

What was wrong with her?

Lying there, with the sun warming her face, bits and pieces of last night came back to her. She had made coq au vin for dinner and had talked to Clark about how to select wine.

As a matter of fact, she had drunk some wine, too. Quite a bit, she recalled ruefully. Hadn't she gotten up from the table to go for more? But she hadn't been able to stand. Then Clark picked her up and carried her... The full memory of last night snapped into place with awful clarity. Her cheeks burned red with shame.

Never in her life had she acted so wanton and disgraceful. When she recalled some of the provocative things she had said, she believed she could never face Clark. Neither, however, could she stay in her room and hide forever. She was going to have to confront him sooner or later.

Slowly, stalling for time, she rose.

Half an hour later, she was dressed. Moving gingerly because of her headache, she made her way downstairs. If she was lucky, Clark would be out working on his car.

She wasn't lucky. She met him at the bottom of the stairs. He was wearing his old work clothes, and his face was red from the outdoors. Felicity grasped the newel post for moral support.

"Good morning," she said gravely.

"Good morning?" His gaze flicked to the grandfather clock. "Good afternoon," he amended with a smile.

"I didn't intend to sleep so late." She wondered if he realized she was being cool to cover her awkwardness.

"Hard to get up with a hangover, isn't it?" His smile was laced with sympathy.

Felicity knew he was trying to put her at ease, but the memory of their fiery embrace was too vivid to allow her to relax. She should never have drunk so much. As if to reinforce that thought, a sudden fierce throbbing in her head assaulted her. She rubbed her temple.

"Got a headache?" he asked.

"Yes," she admitted.

"I've had a few of those myself. They can be rough. The guys in prison used to make home brew out of bread, fruit, anything. Once we made a bucket of some really rancid stuff, and the guard found it. He gave us our choice of being turned in or drinking it. We drank it." He chuckled. "I was sick for three days afterward."

Felicity stared. How could he laugh about something so appalling? More than ever, she felt the wideness of the gulf between them.

Yet last night, she had been ready to surrender to him. The memory brought a flush back to her face. His kisses had spread a hot, sensual glow over her. Even now, with his body showing lean in a pair of jeans and an old sweatshirt, she felt something flutter inside her.

Her reaction startled her. It was not often she was so strongly affected by a man, and she didn't want to be with Clark Fielding.

The sound of the phone ringing provided a welcome interruption. "Excuse me." Releasing her tight grip on the newel post, she hurried into the parlor to answer it. She caught it on the third ring.

"Hello, Felicity. Stewart here."

His accent was upper crust, full of country-club polish. His voice provided a measure of comfort. She had known Stewart since childhood. With Stewart, she did not feel confused or unsure of how to act.

"Hello, Stewart," she said warmly.

"I thought I might run up to visit you this afternoon if you're not busy. We could have dinner at that quaint little place in Provincetown."

Felicity could picture him sitting in his posh law office surrounded by expensive cherry paneling, his chair tipped back as he spoke. It would be good to escape from the inn for a while.

"I'd like that, Stewart."

"Excellent, I'm going to try to get out of town before the Friday-night traffic gets bad."

She had forgotten that today was Friday, the evening of Clark's date. Or perhaps she had chosen not to remember. The thought of him smiling across the table at an attractive woman unsettled her.

Was it because of that that Felicity heard herself injecting added enthusiasm into her voice? "I'll look forward to seeing you, Stewart."

Later, as she changed into a swirling blue skirt with matching self-tie blouse, she thought about Stewart. He was thoughtful, well-bred and charming, and he was considered a very good catch. A lot of women would love to be going out to dinner with him this evening.

She reminded herself of that later when she heard Clark drive away. His car sounded noisy and in need of further work.

Resolutely ignoring the fact she would rather be with him than Stewart, she applied blush to her paler-than-usual cheeks. She didn't need any eye shadow; her eyes were a bright, unhappy blue.

Half an hour later Stewart's Porsche purred noiselessly into the yard. She met him at the door with a smile, trying to ignore the fact her head still ached from last night's overindulgence.

Gallant as always, he kissed her cheek. "You're looking lovely."

As he helped her with her coat, she wondered what she would feel if Stewart kissed her with passion. Would she experience the same molten glow as she had felt with Clark last night? It would have been so easy to put the question to the test. All she had to do was turn in his arms and lift her mouth in invitation. But, of course, she didn't. She was far too reserved to do that.

On the drive to Provincetown, they talked about mutual friends.

They dined at Mariner's Bay, an expensive restaurant with portholes instead of windows looking out onto rippling, moonlit water. The wine was perfect and Stewart was courteously attentive. But Felicity was restless, unable to fix her attention. Twice she had to ask him to repeat something because she hadn't been listening.

"You seem preoccupied tonight, Felicity," he noted.

She offered an apologetic smile. "I'm afraid I had too much wine last night. I'm still feeling the effects."

His eyes twinkled. "I've been there more than once myself. I remember my first year at Yale, some friends and I . . ."

As she listened, she couldn't help noticing that Stewart's drinking tales took place at Yale. Clark's had happened in prison. Not that she needed further proof of how far Clark was removed from her world. So why had she fallen into his arms last night? Even drunk, she wouldn't have done that if she hadn't felt something.

But that was an issue she couldn't allow herself to examine. Pushing it to the back of her mind, she tried to concentrate on a court case Stewart was discussing.

They had a wonderful cherries jubilee dessert, then strolled along the quaint streets of Provincetown and out the boardwalk stretching over the dark water. The stars glittered brightly. Felicity steadfastly ignored the romantic backdrop of the evening and kept the conversation impersonal.

If Stewart was disappointed that the evening wasn't cozier, he was too much of a gentleman to show it. On the way back to the bed and breakfast she wondered what Clark's evening had been like.

* * *

Saturday morning, Clark returned from jogging just as a blue pickup pulled into the yard. Two men emerged from the cab. They took rakes and a roll of plastic garbage bags out of the bed and began raking.

Shaking his head, Clark walked into the house and up the stairs. Why was Felicity paying to have such easy work done when she could do it herself? He knew she could not afford to pay laborers.

"Mind your own business, buddy," he told himself as he peeled his clothes off and left them in a pile on the bathroom floor. He stepped into the shower.

While the warm water splashed over him, he mulled things over in his mind. His dinner with Lauren had been pleasant. She had told him at the outset she was seeing someone seriously. That had relieved him. He had come to see her as a friend and was glad she reciprocated those feelings.

But it had been good to get out, and he had been impressed with how practical Lauren was about money. Lauren worked as a secretary for an accounting firm, but she had begun taking night courses to earn her CPA. Lauren, he was sure, would not hire workers she could not afford.

But Felicity had grown up accustomed to money, and, unfortunately, had no idea how to manage it. Which was why she was in financial trouble with the bed and breakfast.

He hated to think of the inn closing. In the short time he had been there, he had come to like the old house. Clark would never have said so to Felicity, but he thought of the expensive rug on the floor of the blue room where he slept as *his*. He felt possessive about the brass bed. Maybe because he had never had a real home, this place felt special to him. He even enjoyed fixing things around it.

Besides, if he didn't, she was going to go under that much faster by hiring people to do the work.

Stepping out of the shower, he dried himself, dressed and went downstairs. Her finances weren't his affair, he knew, but someone needed to give Felicity advice.

She was leaning against the kitchen counter leafing through recipe books when he walked in. Her simple cotton skirt showed the outline of her thighs. Her legs were crossed at the ankles in a way he found particularly feminine. He tried not to stare at her legs.

"There are some men outside raking," he said brusquely.

She looked at him quizzically. "Yes, I know."

He ran a hand through his still-damp hair. "Look, I don't mean to interfere, but I know you're strapped for money. Hiring those men seems like an unnecessary expense."

"But the yard has to be raked."

"*You* could do it. Or for that matter, get a couple of high-school boys."

Felicity frowned. ''Boys? What sort of job would boys do? One gets what one pays for, you know.''

He didn't know whether to smile or scowl at her naïveté. He thought again that Felicity Simmons might know about manners, but she had a lot to learn about money.

''When it comes to raking a yard, almost anyone can do it. Besides, paying more doesn't guarantee a better job.''

She closed the cookbook and slipped it back onto the shelf above her antique pine writing table. His words contradicted everything she had been taught from childhood. Gram had always hired the best. But then, she admitted, Gram could afford it. And there had also been a snob factor in having the most expensive caterers in town pull up in front of the grand house on Beacon Hill.

''There are a lot of ways you could cut expenses,'' he continued.

Felicity worked the tips of her fingers back and forth across the time-worn pine. Even with Clark's payments and what she was making from piano lessons, money was still tight. If he had some suggestions, it was in her interest to be open to them.

''What do you recommend?'' she asked simply.

''I'd have to sit down and go over the books to know exactly where you could cut back.''

''We could do that sometime.'' A bead of water from the shower lingered on his cheek and she watched it. The firm bone structure of his face stood out even more with his wet hair combed down flat against his skull.

"How about now?" he suggested.

"Well, I suppose we could—"

"Fine," he said briskly.

Ten minutes later, they were installed in the parlor at a cabriole-legged desk with a ledger book spread out before them. Clark pulled his chair up close and peered at the book. He seemed unaware his knee brushed hers, but she was very aware of the pressure and warmth of it. The scent of spicy aftershave wafted over to her and distracted her from the columns of numbers. Did he still think about the passionate kisses they had shared in her room?

But Clark seemed intent on the book as he skimmed through the figures. "It looks like someone is coming once a month to clean the furnace filter. Why?"

"I assume it needed it. The man said it did."

A snort of disgust was his reply. "And what are all these checks to a pest-control service? Are you having trouble with roaches?"

"No. That's preventive maintenance."

"Dump the pest people," he said shortly.

He sounded so definite, as if life would continue to run without service people. But to Felicity they represented security. "The house will fall to rack and ruin if no one takes care of it," she objected.

"Don't be ridiculous. A house doesn't need that kind of attention constantly."

Felicity bit back an argument, determined to listen with an open mind. "Go on."

Clark made several more observations, including a suggestion she turn down the hot-water heater to save money. Finally, he closed the book and looked her straight in the eye.

"You are being taken advantage of. You're paying to have things done that are unnecessary or that you could do yourself."

"As you may recall, I tried and nearly got myself killed," she said tartly.

"It's true you have to be careful, but you certainly can't get hurt raking the front yard."

Silently, she reflected on what he had said. Considering that she owed an alarming number of people, perhaps she should get rid of some of the workers. Just because she had grown up with gardeners didn't mean she could afford them. To most people, they were a luxury; she must begin to think of them that way, too.

He pushed his chair back. Immediately she was aware his knee no longer pressed against hers, and a flicker of regret worked its way through her.

"I wish to thank you, Clark, for the time and trouble you've taken on my account and to—"

He grinned.

"Did I say something wrong?"

"Forget the long speech. Just say 'thanks.'"

"Thank you." She was uncomfortably aware of how stuffy she must have sounded.

"It's nothing. By the way, I think I did everything properly last night."

Including kissing his date at the door when he took her home? Felicity wondered. Had they laughed together and made plans to see each other again?

"I'm glad the lessons are paying off," she said curtly.

She felt moody and irritable when she went into the kitchen to begin preparations for dinner.

The next morning Felicity rose determined to take Clark's advice to heart. She would begin by painting the ceiling of the front porch. She had actually known people who did their own painting so it surely could not be *that* difficult.

Step one was to go into town and buy paint. Once inside the creaking old hardware store, she selected a dark green of the most expensive brand. The higher cost was worth it, she reasoned, because it was sure to last longer. More expensive things always did, didn't they? On the way out of town, she stopped at a trendy woman's dress store and bought a pair of ivory-colored painter's pants and a blue calico blouse. She had to have *something* to paint in.

Back at the house, she changed into her new clothes, pulled her honey-blond hair back into a ponytail and got the small stepladder out of the small shed behind the house. It, thank heavens, was light enough and short enough to be manageable. She brought it to the front porch, opened a can of paint, stirred it and set it on the metal shelf on the ladder.

Then she climbed up, dipped the brush into the paint and applied the first stroke. The fresh green paint made the old gray ceiling look particularly dingy. Inspired, she applied more green. And then a third brushful.

Things were going along well until she splattered some glistening drops on the floor.

"Rats." Frowning, she started to descend the ladder to wipe it up. More paint dripped off the brush and formed an army of green dots on the floor.

Well, the old brown floor didn't look that great, either. Why not paint it, too?

Satisfied with that idea, she stayed on the ladder and continued her task. It was almost impossible to paint overhead without dripping, she noted unhappily as her new outfit became speckled with green. Then she sprinkled some green on the white window frame. It could stand to be painted as well, she decided, and green trim would look nice against the white clapboard walls of the porch. Abandoning the ceiling, she climbed off the ladder and concentrated her efforts on the window frame.

Unfortunately, some paint got on the swing, too. She didn't notice it until the drops had begun to harden. Even though she rubbed them vigorously with a rag, she couldn't remove them. It looked as if she would have to paint the swing, too. The job was getting out of hand, and she was beginning to panic

when Clark appeared from around the side of the
house.

He stopped on the top step, frowning. "What are
you doing?"

"Painting," she answered with a touch of defi-
ance. What did he mean by asking what she was
doing? He was the one who had suggested being
more self-reliant.

"I see that. Why didn't you put down papers?"

"Papers?"

"On the floor, so you wouldn't get paint on it."

She felt self-conscious under his frown. "That
didn't occur to me. I decided to go ahead and paint
the floor instead."

"You're painting the window frame, too?"

"I thought it might look nice in green." She'd be
darned if she was going to admit she hadn't originally intended to paint it.

He sighed. "You're making a lot of extra work for
yourself. Wait here."

He was back a few minutes later with a stack of
newspapers and a can of turpentine. With spare efficiency, he spread papers, then stepped past her and
raised and lowered the window.

"What are you doing?" she asked.

"If you don't move it once in a while, the paint
will dry and seal it shut."

"Oh." Feeling foolish, she defended herself, "I
was following *your* advice to be more self-sufficient."

"You get credit for trying," he said in a gentler voice. "I'm sorry if I seemed critical. But there are some things you have to know to do the job right."

He knelt on the floor and began working at removing the splatters with a rag soaked in turpentine. "Don't worry. Everything can be taken care of." His words were quiet and soothing, the way she sometimes talked to skittish horses at the saddle club. Felicity didn't know whether to be pleased or insulted by his tone.

He rose. "Do you have another brush?"

"Yes, I bought two. The other one is in the package in the corner."

When he opened the sack, the receipt fell out. Clark glanced at it, then let out a long, low whistle. "Judging from these prices, there must be a bar of gold bullion in the bottom of each paint can."

She lifted her chin proudly. "I may have paid a little more, but it's quality paint. I won't have to do the job again for a long time."

"I hope not," he muttered. He opened a can, climbed up the ladder and began feathering smooth strokes over the old gray paint. No drops fell from his brush. She was impressed in spite of herself.

Quietly, she turned to go about her own work. Minutes ticked by and her wounded pride began to heal. It was comforting to have someone helping, especially someone who knew what he was doing.

More time passed and she became increasingly aware of Clark's presence. His lower half was at eye level. As she ran her brush back and forth across the smooth wooden swing, she noticed his jeans tapering down from narrow hips to strong thighs and long legs. When he twisted to the side, the view of his male bottom reminded her that she had noticed his backside the first time she met him. He had also, she recalled, turned and caught her in mid-stare.

The memory made her smile. She glanced up and saw Clark smiling back at her.

"It's not such bad work, is it?" he asked.

"Not at all." She was glad he didn't know the real reason for her smile.

They continued their work in companionable silence. After a time, Clark began to softly whistle a pleasant, upbeat melody. She was paying more attention to it than her work when she dipped the brush into the can and brought it out again.

"Darn!" Felicity exclaimed as a huge glob of paint slopped onto the floor.

Clark descended the ladder. "Here, let me show you something." He wrapped a large, warm hand over hers. Guiding her movements, he put the tip of the brush into the can, lifted it and slid it along the rim of the can until most of the paint fell off. "Now, stroke in long, even motions like this."

Felicity felt his knuckles flexing to direct her hand.

"You blend with light pressure," he lectured.

"I see." But she was paying little heed. She was smelling the turpentine on his fingers and feeling the rough texture of his skin. When, she wondered, was the last time he had touched a woman intimately?

If she hadn't looked up into his eyes at that moment she might have continued working without incident. But she did look up and saw that his eyes were dark with inner struggle. It wasn't often that she could read Clark, but at the moment she was sure of both his desire and uncertainty.

She could have moved away, and the moment would have passed. But she remained where she was. Waiting. Willing him to touch her.

Slowly, he lifted his hands and smoothed back wisps of hair from either side of her face. His hands came to rest above her ears and he left them there, holding her head motionless as he bent toward her.

She didn't have a wealth of experience kissing men, but she realized he wasn't sure of himself. She wasn't sure either. He was so terribly masculine that she was almost fearful of him. And he, she knew, was nervous because he had been away from women for so long.

He cupped his hands around her upper arms and slowly pulled her to her feet, wrapping her close against him. She felt urgency in the tightened muscles of his body, but his mouth remained tentative. She wanted to put her arms around him, but her own reserve made her keep them straight at her side.

Except for those brief moments the other night, she knew it had been a long time since Clark had caressed a woman. He was holding back his desire. She wondered if it would reassure him to realize her own experience with men was limited. Would it help him to know she longed for him to kiss her with the intensity of the other night?

Perhaps he read the invitation in her eyes, or perhaps his own needs overcame hesitation. At any rate, his soft kiss suddenly became one of hard possession. He parted her lips with the insistent tip of his tongue, kissing her with tormented need.

She was startled by the intensity of his passion. He clamped her against him until she felt every inch of his body. If she had been in any doubt about his longing, she was convinced of it now.

His tongue thrust inside her mouth suggestively. A voluptuous shiver of response ran through her.

Slowly Clark rubbed his hands down her arms. His touch pulled the strength from her, leaving her weak in its wake. When he reached her fingers, he curled each one closed until her small hands formed fists. Then he covered each of her hands with his large ones and pulled her toward him until she was off balance, supported only by his body. She felt the wanting in him even more distinctly.

The signs of his yearning increased her own, and when his tongue darted into her mouth again, she wrapped her tongue around it, holding it captive.

He emitted a low, guttural groan that reverberated into her mouth. She hadn't known anything could be so erotic.

Lost in a world of the senses, she luxuriated in the feel of his male body against her feminine one. She inhaled the scent of new paint that clung to him. She heard his unsteady breathing mingling with her own uneven breaths. She felt his heartbeat thumping in counterpoint to the quick rhythm of her own. Opening her eyes, she saw the stark wanting in his eyes. She felt his hands cover the swell at the sides of her breasts.

Suddenly, she had a sharp picture of those same hands wrapped around the cold bars of a prison cell and she tensed.

Clark must have felt it, for he drew back, a question in his eyes.

He had been in prison, she thought wildly, as she pulled further away. He was a criminal. What was she doing encouraging him to kiss her?

Yet somewhere inside her she knew that was only an excuse. Her real fear was of abandoning herself to passion.

# Seven

Clark stepped away. Left to stand alone, Felicity felt
the unsteadiness of her knees. She wanted to say
something but didn't trust her voice. Instead, she
brushed back her disheveled hair and stood silently.

He watched her a moment in square-jawed silence, his eyes an impassive pewter. "I suppose we
ought to continue painting." He was no longer
looking at her.

Regaining her poise, at least outwardly, she
matched his expressionless tone. "Yes, I suppose we
should."

Her body still tingled with little volts of electricity
his kisses had generated. A flush of passion still
singed her cheeks.

Nearby, she sensed Clark painting with grim efficiency. She wondered if his body also glowed with the aftereffects.

"Felicity?"

"Yes?"

"All of a sudden, I can't paint worth a damn. Would you get a rag and wipe up those drops near the corner?"

"Yes, of course." It gave her satisfaction to know his hand was not so steady now. Somehow that relieved the strain on her, and she began to relax.

Time passed and the torrid moments in his arms seemed less real, like something she had imagined rather than something that had happened.

As they worked silently, she became so at ease that she didn't notice time slipping away. It was not until the last light of day failed that she realized how late it was.

"Goodness," she said, "it's time to start dinner, and I haven't given a thought to what to have."

Clark looked up. "Why don't we drive into town and grab something?"

"I suppose we could," she said doubtfully. She thought of dinner as a formal occasion that required china and silver. She knew other people dined on hamburgers or pizzas but she rarely did.

"It will save you going to so much trouble for just the two of us. I'll buy." He put the lids back on the paint cans and gathered up rags. "I'll wash the brushes out in the basement while you get ready."

Felicity nodded. Most of her life had been structured. Because she was not in the habit of doing things on the spur of the moment, the spontaneity of the idea appealed to her.

Leaving Clark behind, she hurried upstairs to change out of her paint-splattered clothes and into a feminine apricot blouse and matching wraparound skirt. She paused only long enough to brush her hair, ignoring the little flecks of green in it. Then she rolled a gloss of pastel lipstick on her lips.

By the time she arrived downstairs, Clark was waiting by the door.

"I can drive," he offered.

"Okay." They walked to the garage side by side. Their fingers didn't touch, but the companionable air between them made her feel she could easily slip her hand into his. It was a sense of friendship that made her feel warm and happy.

He held the door of his old car for her, then got in and started the engine.

"It's still a little noisy," he apologized. "I haven't finished fine-tuning it."

Felicity thought of the elegant purr of Stewart's car and realized she would not rather be in it. She was content to relax back on the faded blue vinyl seat next to Clark.

Darkness had fallen, and a full moon cast a pearly glow over the landscape, making the bearberry covering the ground along the road shimmer. Off to the right, she saw the water of the bay rippling out into the darkness.

"Any particular place you'd like to eat?" Clark asked.

They were on the edge of Wellfleet, headed into town past the weathered saltbox houses.

"No, I don't eat out often." When she did, it was at fashionable restaurants like the one she and Stewart had gone to in Provincetown or to trendy Boston establishments.

"Let's try this one." He spun the car into the parking lot of a restaurant boldly advertising *Good Eats*.

The inside proved to be everything the outside had hinted at. Formica tables lined one side of the room; a long counter with stools formed the other half. Several diners dotted the counter.

Clark glanced around with an air of satisfaction. "Looks okay, don't you think?"

"It's unpretentious," she agreed. Did that sound snobbish? She added, "I like it."

They sat at a table in the corner, ordered catfish and hush puppies from a pert waitress and settled back to wait.

"I want to thank you for your help today," Felicity said. "I really appreciate it."

He shrugged. "Forget it. You're doing me a favor, too."

"But you're *paying* me."

Both leaned back as the waitress slid two steaming plates of food onto the table. Then he hunched forward again, a visible tautness settling over his shoulders.

"You're not just teaching me manners. I could learn that from a book."

She watched him, her brows drawn together in confusion.

"Where I spent the last three years, self-confidence wasn't exactly stressed. It scares the hell out of me to think of working with people who know a lot more about how to act than I do."

"You're scared?" She leaned forward, elbows on the table and Gram Simmons's good etiquette forgotten. "It's hard to imagine that. You don't seem like you're afraid of anything."

He smiled ruefully. "I learned to act tough in prison. I'm an ex-con and people are going to know that. But I don't want them to look down at me because I'm rough and unmannered."

Felicity swelled with indignation. How dare anyone look down at him and make him feel uncomfortable? Then she realized she had done it herself. So had her grandmother. For a man with Clark's pride, that must have hurt.

In no time at all the waitress was back, clearing the plates and reciting a litany of desserts. "Care for pie? Pecan? Lemon meringue? Coconut? Gooseberry?"

"No, thanks." Clark reached behind to pull out his wallet. "Why don't we go for a walk on the beach?" he suggested.

"I'd like that."

They left the restaurant and ambled along the water's edge without speaking. The cone-shaped dunes made a silent backdrop in the moonlight. Soon, Felicity knew, ice-flecked waves spawned by one of winter's "nor'easters," would beat against the frozen land. But for now, it was unseasonably temperate. The breeze was cool, but not unpleasant. She was glad to be here with Clark in a way she was seldom glad to be anywhere.

"Did you know the granite that forms the basement rock here identically matches the rock in Morocco? Before the continents separated, the two were one land mass."

She blinked at him. "How do you know that?"

He shrugged. "I read a lot in prison."

Their feet made gentle thuds in the sand. He had shortened his stride to fit hers so that they moved in time with each other.

"What was it like?" She wasn't used to asking personal questions, but she felt close to Clark at the moment. It was important to her to understand him better.

He looked up at the black sky, as if the answer were written there. "Hard. Bleak. You always want to be out. Sometimes it eats at you to think your life is slipping away while you're locked behind bars."

Felicity heard the pain in his words. "Why were you in there?" she asked slowly.

"I was involved in a burglary. Drove the getaway car." He laughed shortly. "The first thing I did in prison was tell everyone I met that I wasn't guilty. What a fool I was. Every guy in there was singing the same tune."

She turned to face him, trying to see past the uncertain moonlight to read every nuance in his face. His smile was tight and brittle.

"If you were innocent, couldn't you appeal? A good lawyer could have—"

"Felicity, the system doesn't always work the way you think it does. Sometimes it only works that way for people who have money and influence."

"Meaning me? No, don't answer that." Because she didn't want to argue or put anything between them, she grasped at the first new subject that came to mind. "What do you think of the Celtics this year?"

He laughed. It was a rich, rippling sound that played across his vocal chords in an astonishingly appealing way.

She smiled. "I guess that wasn't an exceptionally smooth change of subject."

"The intentions were good, and that's what counts." He reached out and took her hand, locking his big fingers around her smaller ones. They walked in silence, hands swinging gently between them.

She was in no hurry to leave, and she felt regret when he finally led the way back to the car.

The motion of the warm car and the soft classical music quickly made her drowsy. Her head began to list to one side, and she fought to keep her eyes open. But she felt herself sinking.

Some time later someone touched her shoulder. "Felicity?"

Blinking, she awoke to find herself in front of her house.

Clark came around and opened her door, putting a steadying hand around her arm. She was still sleepy enough that she felt tempted to lean her head on his shoulder. But she didn't.

Inside the house, she shed her coat and tossed it carelessly into a corner chair. At the moment, she was more intent on getting into bed than worrying about hangers.

"Good night," she mumbled.

Stifling a yawn, she padded upstairs to her bedroom. In her half-awake state, she knocked over a lamp and broke the light bulb. Bleary-eyed, she bent to pick up the pieces.

"Ouch!" The quick, sharp points of the glass sank into her finger and blood surfaced.

Clark appeared in her doorway. "What's wrong?"

"I cut myself," she mumbled.

"Sit on the bed and let me see if there's any glass in there."

Holding her throbbing finger, she sank onto the rose print of her bedspread. As he explored the cut with callused fingers, she watched his face. It was odd to think that her first impression had been how hard he looked. At that moment his expression was gentle. Even tender. It awakened something inside her and made her want to reach out and smooth back the dark hair the wind had scattered across his forehead.

"Seems fine," he pronounced as he wrapped a tissue around it.

He looked at her then. She gazed back helplessly, a prisoner to the longing beginning to overtake her.

"I can do one of two things right now—leave or stay," he said huskily.

She nodded mutely, willing him to stay.

He must have decided that, too, for his mouth came down atop hers with fierce purpose. It was a kiss all the more potent for the length of time it had been building. She sensed the pent-up need in the questing way his lips moved over hers.

He wrapped his arms around her with enough force to throw her off balance. She fell back onto the bed, and he followed her down. The weight of his body pressed against hers. She felt the rock-hard muscles of his thighs against her legs.

His mouth continued to cover hers with ravenous kisses, like a man devouring a meal after being too long without food. She responded with the same urgent hunger, willingly opening her lips when his tongue sought the soft interior of her mouth.

His splayed hands dug into her back, pressing her nearer while his lips continued to massage hers with rising need. As she clung to him, she opened her mouth to his probing tongue. She was smothering in the very maleness of him. His heart pounded loud and fast against her chest. His arms were cages of iron, trapping her against his unyielding body where she inhaled the musky, earthy scent of sweat.

While his body hardened, hers grew soft and pliable. Her breasts became tender and sensitive pressed up against the cliff of his chest. Her lips felt swollen, ripe with kissing and aching to be kissed.

His hands slid down to her breasts, and he began to rub with tantalizing vigor. Everything he did, he would do completely, she sensed. That led her to the ultimate thought that he would make love in a way that would leave her speechless.

Her body yearned to experience that. If there were passages of her mind that harbored doubts, she blocked them, refusing to follow any course but the one unfolding before her. Her breathing was quick and uneven, struggling to keep pace with the frantic beating of her heart. Her whole body felt heated, glowing from the fire burning within.

And still his mouth plundered hers searchingly. Their tongues danced and mated, slid together and apart, seduced and seducing in a way that made her quiver.

She was alive to his every movement. When his fingers slipped down the front of her apricot blouse, she felt the buttons falling open. He impatiently pushed the blouse off. Then she felt work-hardened fingers on the French silk of her bra.

She could feel his haste. His need. The years without a woman had been too long, and he was straining against the bounds of desire. In a moment her blouse lay in a dainty heap on the floor.

Even the most passionate need couldn't make her forget scruples entirely. She could not contemplate making love because of mere physical attraction. Far greater forces were at work here. Close in his arms like this, she felt herself opening up and drawing him nearer to her heart.

He must have sensed her thoughts, for his mouth grew softer on hers. His kisses remained intense, but now they were full of gentle persuasion, as if he wanted to give as well as take.

That was evident in the caring way he removed the rest of her clothes. And then he hesitated, lying completely motionless on the bed beside her.

She waited with straining impatience.

"Felicity, it's been so long—" He broke off. "I'm afraid I'll—"

"Shhh." Lifting a hand, she stroked his hair. "I don't think that's possible. I want you to touch me." Her fingers skimmed over the razor stubble of his chin.

He raised up on one elbow to rain a torrent of kisses on her. And then his hands began to search.

Because he hadn't been with a woman for so long, his fingers trembled with his first touches of her bare skin. He stroked her breasts and then the satiny interior of her thighs.

"So soft," he whispered, his voice breaking.

For all his hesitation, it was soon apparent he understood a woman's body very well. She felt the skill of his hands' subtle arousal. With just the right touches and pressure, he stirred her to the point of vibrant excitement.

He murmured rough, incoherent phrases as his hands worked their magic. If she didn't understand the words, she could tell the intent as he touched her with growing intimacy.

Then he joined his body to hers. His kisses and caresses became more intense, soaked with intimacy. Her fingers traced over the thin sheen of sweat on his bare back. He felt hot, and his breathing was ragged against the shell of her ear.

He began to sway against her.

She scaled walls of pure sensation until she was breathless with longing and poised on the edge of something awe-inspiring. And scary. She had never before let go completely and abandoned herself to pure sensations. Something held her back now.

Then he clutched her tightly against him. Opening her eyes, she watched him rebound from the intensity of the moment. His eyelids were half closed, shielding the sated passion in his eyes. His whole body relaxed. She felt the tenseness ripple out of the strong muscles on his back. It was a powerful, moving feeling for Felicity to have inspired such a moment, and for that she was profoundly grateful.

He kissed her quietly, touching lips already swollen with his kisses. Then he fitted her into the crook of his shoulder. Safe there and warmed by the heat of his body, she fell asleep.

Felicity awoke the next morning to the sound of running water and realized that Clark was taking a shower. That meant he had already been out jogging.

The sound of his off-key humming brought a smile to her lips. Thoughts of last night softened that smile.

He was in the kitchen by the time she was dressed and downstairs. For one moment, while his back was to her, she wasn't sure how he would respond to her, or if it would be awkward between them. Then he turned and his face lit with pleasure.

"Good morning. I made coffee."

"You didn't have to do that."

"I might as well get used to doing things for myself. I'll have to soon."

In the pleasure of last night, she had forgotten he would be leaving. His words were a sharp reminder. Suddenly she felt bereft, already missing him. In the short time he had been here, she had grown accustomed to hearing his footsteps and to having his company at dinner. Even when tension stood between them, she had not felt alone. But in less than a week, he would be gone.

He finished his coffee. "Guess I better get out and do some work on the car." He paused to touch his lips to hers before leaving through the back door.

Standing at the kitchen window, she watched him walk to the garage. The wind riffled through his dark hair and he moved with extra vigor today.

"What did you think was going to happen, Felicity?" she asked aloud. Yesterday and last night had not changed the course of events. It might have changed the way she looked at him, and at herself, but he was still leaving.

But endings were negative, and right now she was unwilling to be anything but positive. This didn't have to be a permanent parting, she told herself. He was only moving to Boston. She refused to consider anything except the smiles they had exchanged and how she had felt with him last night. All her thoughts were centered on Clark.

It was an effort to concentrate on piano lessons when Melanie Sawyer arrived to go up and down the scales. Later Kevin Porter sat with chubby legs dangling and his tongue squeezed between his front teeth while he practiced. She remained distracted, watching out the window for Clark.

After the lessons, she put lamb chops out to thaw. If he had only a few more days here, she wanted to make them as special as possible. She wanted the food to be perfect, and she wanted to impart every bit of knowledge she had so he would feel at ease in the world.

That evening she dressed in a soft apricot sweater dress and set the table with a full barrage of silverware. Candles flickered in crystal holders.

Clark walked into the room and stopped.

Felicity bit her bottom lip, waiting for his reaction to the romantic backdrop.

He put her at ease by nodding approval. "Something smells great. I can't figure out if it's the cook or the food."

"I hope it's both." She would never have said that to any other man, but with Clark it felt right. With him, a lot of things seemed right.

He held her chair, then sat down across from her. She thought he looked wonderful in a gray pullover sweater that accented his eyes.

He swept a hand over the assembled silverware. "What's this?"

"I'm going to explain about silverware. We'll start with the knives." A row of five stood to the right of each plate. She picked one and held it up. "Never use the knife located near the butter dish to spread butter." Felicity smiled and almost forgot the subject.

He grinned. "Yes?"

"Er, you use it to put a pat on your side plate, then use your bread knife for putting the butter on the bread," she continued, striving for a steadiness to her voice that seemed to escape her. "At a very proper affair, it should either be lying diagonally across your side plate or the last one to your right in a row of knives."

"Why go to all that trouble? Why can't you use the same knife to butter your bread, cut your meat and point at the guy across the table during an argument?"

"Because it's not done," she said pertly, responding to the teasing glint in his eye. "If your hostess asks you to keep your flatware for the next course, do as she says. Put the fork with the tines facing down and rest the top of your knife in the arc it forms so you don't dirty the tablecloth. Like so." She picked up another in the row of knives. "Now this one is—"

"You look very pretty tonight."

"Thank you." She was quickly losing the impetus to discuss silverware. It was far more intriguing to banter with him and gaze into his eyes and feel his smile cuddling her.

She wished it could have remained that way. But the sound of the doorbell cut into their conversation.

# Eight

---

"Excuse me." Putting her damask napkin aside, Felicity went to open the front door. The man who stood beneath the yellow glow of the porch light wore a stained gray sweatshirt and a visored hat and smoked a cigarette. He was short and stocky, he glanced about furtively, and he made her uneasy. If he was looking for a room, he was going to have to search elsewhere.

"May I help you?" she asked in her most unencouraging blue-blood accent.

"Is Clark Fielding here?"

She hesitated. "May I tell him who is calling?"

"Bruce." He ground the cigarette out on the porch floor.

"I'll call him."

. Instead of waiting in the hall, he followed her into the dining room. "Hello, buddy," he said quietly to Clark.

Felicity watched Clark push back his chair and rise. "Bruce. When did you get out?"

Neither man moved toward the other, but she sensed it was an emotional reunion, and that this was someone who mattered to Clark. She looked at the taut, hard lines of the stranger's face and felt a quiver of worry.

"Two days ago." Bruce glanced warily at her, then back to Clark.

"Got a job yet?" Clark asked.

"No," he said tightly.

Again Felicity saw Bruce cut a hard look in her direction. She wondered if her distrust showed so plainly in her face or if he was suspicious of everyone.

Remembering his lessons on introductions, Clark said uncomfortably, "Felicity, this is Bruce Morgan. Bruce, this is Felicity Simmons. She's my landlady."

The term made her sound like someone on the periphery of his life. She was startled at how much the term "landlady" hurt.

"Ma'am." Bruce nodded curtly in her direction, then turned back to Clark. "Can we go somewhere for a beer?"

"Sure." Clark pushed his chair in.

She sensed a bond between the two men that excluded her and felt suddenly like an outsider.

"You don't mind, do you, Felicity?" Clark asked as an afterthought.

She shook her head. But she did mind. Very much. She wanted him to remain with her, and she yearned to feel the closeness that had been shattered with Bruce's arrival. Most of all, she didn't want Clark to be with this man who made her so uneasy.

But even as those thoughts ran through her mind, the two men started from the room.

Then she heard the front door close, and she was alone among the carefully laid out place settings and the gleaming silverware. She pushed her plate aside, no longer hungry.

Where were Clark and Bruce going and what would they say to each other? Would they talk about old times in prison or discuss their futures? Or would they plan a surefire way to grab a lot of money without getting caught? "I know this guy who works in a bank, and he has all the details on the safe and..."

She had seen reunions like this one in dozens of old movies. Then the characters hadn't been real people to her. Now one of them was someone she knew.

Or did she?

She had not even wanted Bruce in her house, yet he was a friend of Clark's. And both men were ex-convicts.

Rising, she paced. Might not Clark, at any time, return to crime? He said he had a job in Boston, but how did she know that was true? He might have been waiting all along for Bruce to show up. They could have a crime already planned. For all she knew, they were out committing it right now. An edge of panic rose into her throat.

"Calm down, Felicity," she said aloud. Putting her palms on the cool ledge of the windowsill, she looked out into the night. But she remained shaken.

She tried to think of things that had reassured her in the past. She thought about the water lapping against the sand on the beach and of days when the sunshine seemed endless. She thought about last night and how loving and tender Clark had been with her.

Slowly, she slid her fingers back and forth along the cool ledge. She had let him kiss her and hold her so close that she had felt she could lose herself in him. She had let herself believe he was like other men. But he was not.

He had spent time locked up with thieves. He had been branded a criminal, and even though he said he wasn't guilty, she had no way of knowing that. Under those circumstances, how could she allow herself to be anything but skeptical of him?

Yes, she admitted that she wanted to trust him. She almost felt compelled to trust him. But the facts didn't seem to bear that out. Rising she whirled from the dark window, feeling trapped and unhappy.

What was she to do? She had spent last night with Clark. She had begun to feel something for him. She had—yes, she must admit it—looked forward to being with him tonight.

But that was not to be, she realized as she slumped back into her chair. There were too many doubts.

As painful as it might be, she had to put distance between herself and Clark. That would be difficult to do when they were alone in the house. Since no other guests were likely to come, she was going to have to take matters into her own hands.

Forcing herself to rise, she walked into the kitchen and dialed long distance to a friend. She had known Melinda since her Vassar days.

Melinda was quick to hear the ache in her voice. "Is anything wrong?" she demanded.

"I'm a little down. I was wondering if you'd like to come for a visit?"

"I can't be gone long, but I'm free tomorrow. How would it be if I drove up for a short visit?"

"I'd love it."

Clark awoke the next morning with a lot on his mind. His first thought was of Felicity. He had never intended to go to bed with her, but now that he had, powerful feelings had been aroused. The time he had spent with her seemed special, precious in a way few things in his life had ever been.

But he was not blind to the fact she was from a wealthy, privileged class. And he was a man just out of prison.

Sitting at the edge of the bed, he tied his jogging shoes. What was going to happen with them? It hurt to think this was only a fling for both of them. But what more could he expect? Given the circumstances, he was afraid to ask for more.

Then there was the problem of Bruce. His friend was terrified at being on the "outside" after seven years in prison. While he insisted he was glad to be free, Clark could see he was scared.

Clark understood the feelings because he had them himself. In an odd way, there was safety in being locked behind stone walls. Clark was adjusting to life on the outside, though, and he wanted to help Bruce do the same. He just wasn't sure how to accomplish that.

Bruce had rented a room in a rundown section of Boston not far from the seedy "combat zone." He had gone back to Boston because he had an interview for a job as a janitor. Clark hoped the interview went well. Bruce needed the job and the money, but he needed the boost to his ego even more.

After his morning run, Clark went out to work on his car. For some reason, Felicity hadn't been in the kitchen at breakfast time. He quietly made a cup of coffee and carried it out to the garage. If she was sleeping late, he didn't want to disturb her. The telephone was ringing when he returned to the house around noon. Why didn't she answer it?

It was still jangling when he picked up the receiver in the kitchen. "Hello."

"Clark? It's Bruce."

The other man was speaking fast and loud, obviously upset. Clark felt a shadow of worry.

"I didn't get the job."

"That's a tough break," Clark said sympathetically, "but it's not the only job in Boston. You'll find something else before long."

"No, I won't. Nobody wants an ex-con working for them."

"*I* got a job," Clark reminded him.

"Yeah, 'cause you're smart, and you went to college. But I don't even have a high-school education. Who would hire me?"

The depression in his voice worried Clark. He tried for a soothing tone. "Bruce, I'm sure in a day or so—"

"I just wanted you to know if anything happens to me, I've got some money saved up, and I want you to have it."

Alarm shot up Clark's spine. "You're talking crazy. What's going to happen to you?"

"It's not going to get any better. I might as well end things before they get worse."

Clark gripped the phone tighter. "Listen to me, your luck will change. Don't give up because you didn't get the first job."

"It's not just that. It's me. I'm a loser. The world already has enough losers. One less would be a good thing."

"Things aren't as bad as you think. Believe me, life looks the worst right after you get out of prison. It will get better."

"It's no use." Defeat vibrated through the phone.

He looked around desperately. He could call the police in Boston but their arrival might push Bruce over the brink. No, the best thing was to try to get there. "I'm coming down to see you. Don't do anything until I get there. Do you understand?"

"I was better off in prison. At least there I was with my own kind. Out here, I'm a loser. I've got the record to prove it."

"I'll be there as fast as I can."

Slamming down the phone, Clark rushed out to his car, not even bothering to get a coat. Damn! He had the starter out of his car.

He rushed back to the house, calling Felicity's name as the back door slammed behind him. No answer. Grabbing her keys from the gateleg table near the front door, he ran out. He would explain things later. At the moment, he had to get to Boston before Bruce did something foolish.

From her upstairs window, Felicity had watched Clark go jogging and later out to the garage. She had deliberately remained upstairs so she wouldn't come face to face with him. She couldn't handle that yet. Still, she longed to see him, if only from a distance.

Thankfully, Melinda arrived in midmorning. Felicity's friend was a short, plump woman who always claimed to be on the verge of losing twenty pounds. She greeted Felicity with a hard squeeze and a kiss on the cheek.

Over a cup of coffee, Melinda suggested they go out for a drive. "Getting out will cure your blues."

So they went off in Melinda's sports car to explore the little shops around the Cape and to catch up on old friends.

It was good to get out. At times, as they wandered in and out of the quaint little shops in Provincetown, Felicity almost forgot about Clark. Almost.

It was one in the afternoon before they arrived back home. Melinda pulled into the driveway and parked.

Brushing aside the black bangs that hung low on her forehead, she turned to Felicity. "Wasn't your car here when we left?"

"Yes."

"What happened to it?"

"I don't know." She wasn't worried, but she was puzzled as she entered the house. The keys were gone from the drawer where she always kept them. A frown settled over her face. If anyone had taken the keys, Clark would have heard them. Drawing in a fortifying breath, she went upstairs and knocked on Clark's door. There was no answer.

Melinda watched her descend the steps. "Is someone else here?"

"I have a guest in one of the rooms, but he's out at the moment."

"Where was his car parked? I only saw yours when I got here."

"He keeps it in the garage. He's doing some work on it."

Melinda's eyebrows went up. "An overnight guest is working on his car in your garage? That's rather irregular, isn't it?"

"He's been here awhile," Felicity said distractedly. *Where* was her car?

"I don't mean to be an alarmist, but your guest is gone and your car is gone. Could this guy have taken it?"

Felicity chewed at her lower lip. "I don't think so."

"You don't sound very confident."

"Well—" She remembered the Pandora's box of doubts that Bruce's visit had opened inside her. "Maybe Clark is out in the garage." He would be able to explain things.

The two women crossed the yard together. But no one was in the old clapboard garage. Nor was anyone walking along the stretch of beach visible from the yard.

By the time they returned to the house, Felicity was growing sick with foreboding. Bruce had been here last night and now her automobile was gone. Had Clark shown him where the keys were?

"What do you think?" Melinda demanded as they stood inside the back door.

"Maybe Clark borrowed the car." A hard knot of anxiety continued to grow in her stomach. There didn't seem to be a logical reason he would have done that, since his car ran.

"Wouldn't he have left a note?" Melinda countered. "Let's look upstairs in his room and see if he's taken his things."

Unhappily, Felicity led the way upstairs, pushed the door to his room open and went in. The bed was neatly made; his navy-blue jogging clothes were folded and laid at the foot.

Melinda pulled open drawers. "Not much here."

"He didn't have much." Why did she feel compelled to defend Clark when she suspected him herself?

Melinda fixed her with an uncompromising stare. "Exactly what do you know about this guy?"

"He seemed nice enough," she said vaguely.

"There's something you're not saying. I can tell by the way you're acting."

Sighing, Felicity went to look out the window. "He had just gotten out of prison."

"You're not serious!" Melinda's voice changed to wonder. "You *are* serious. Some jailbird steals your car and you're standing here doing nothing."

Why was she doing nothing? Felicity asked herself. Because she wanted to believe it wasn't true. Yet all the evidence indicated otherwise. Her car was gone and Clark was gone. He had kissed her and held her and made love to her. She had wanted that to mean he would not hurt her. Naïvely, she still clung to that hope. It seemed all she had to hold on to.

"Let's give it another hour or so before we do anything," Felicity said. "Maybe he'll be back."

Exasperation added force to Melinda's voice. "Will you be reasonable? The longer we wait, the farther away he can get. He's probably already been gone for hours." Striding out of the room, she headed downstairs. "I'm calling the police."

With the weight of her pain slowing her steps, Felicity followed. "I'll talk," she said heavily. After all, they would need a license-plate number and other specifics that Melinda could not give.

After dialing the police and giving the details of make and model, the female dispatcher asked if she had any idea who might have stolen the car.

Felicity took a deep, steadying breath. "Clark Fielding."

"Can you describe him?"

"Tall, dark hair." And gray eyes that had looked at her with passion, and strong hands that he had used to hold her body against his.

"Do you know where he might have gone?" the dispatcher asked.

"Boston, perhaps." It was where he was from. Or where he told her he was from. Now she had to question everything he had said. And she had to question her feelings for him.

After asking a few more questions, the dispatcher said, "That's all the information we need. We'll put this into the computer."

"Thank you." Felicity replaced the receiver on its cradle. There might still be a mistake, she told herself.

But there wasn't. The next day, after the most restless night she had ever spent, the police called. Her car had been recovered and the thief was being held in jail in Boston.

"Who is he?" she asked woodenly.

"Fielding, Clark. Same one you thought it would be. Ma'am? Are you still there?"

Felicity took a deep breath and forced herself to say, "I'll come get the car."

She was tense and silent during the trip into the Boston suburb.

"I understand that you don't want to talk," Melinda said comfortingly.

But her friend didn't understand at all, Felicity realized. Melinda thought she was worried about her car, but a dent in it was nothing compared to the damage to her emotions. She had let herself believe she could trust Clark. They had painted the porch together, shared meals, walked on the beach, made love. Now her faith had been broken like a fragile vase, and she was cutting herself on the sharp edges of that broken trust.

Finally the long ride was over, and Melinda pulled the car to a stop at the police station. They went inside the grim, institutional building. As she moved zombielike through the corridors, Felicity wondered if this reminded Clark of prison.

Melinda stopped a passing policeman to ask where to go.

They were directed to a deputy prosecutor's office. There they met Mr. Schrems, a fortyish man with the beginnings of a blond mustache. A cigarette seemed to be a permanent fixture on one side of his mouth. He motioned them toward vinyl chairs and picked up a pen, ready to write on a yellow notepad.

Sitting behind his desk, he began, "To help us build a case, I'd like to have your story, Ms. Simmons. Why don't we start by you giving me some background?"

"Background?" Felicity repeated, unable to concentrate while her stomach churned.

"Yes. Mr. Fielding had keys to your car. Did you give them to him or how did he get them?"

"He took them," Melinda answered for her. Her sharp decisiveness was in contrast to Felicity's distraught silence.

Mr. Schrems turned to her. "Where were the keys, Ms. Simmons?"

Melinda spoke again. "In Felicity's house."

"He broke into the house?"

"He lives there," Felicity replied. Agitated, she rose and began to pace. Clark had taken the car, but maybe there was a good reason. After all, he had not stolen anything before. On the contrary, he had helped her around the house by fixing things. There must be a reason he had driven it all the way to Boston without asking her.

He put down his pen and stared at her. "Ms. Simmons, let me ask you something. Is this a lover's quarrel?"

"Of course not!" Melinda replied. "The man is a thief. It's your job to put him back behind bars where he belongs."

Mr. Schrems was still staring at Felicity. "I'm not sure that's what Ms. Simmons wants. Is it?"

She was silent. Clark hadn't taken his belongings so maybe he *had* intended to return. After all, if his intent had been to steal, he would have taken the expensive silverware or her jewelry. Now that she was here, it was beginning to seem more and more like a mistake.

The lawyer exhaled smoke, still keeping the cigarette clamped on one side of his mouth. "The police have gone to a great deal of effort to find your car. It has been through two city police departments and the state police. When we go to this much effort we expect the people who wanted us to do it will at least cooperate. You will testify to the facts of the case, won't you?"

Felicity realized she was in a corner. She was being pushed to press charges, and she wasn't sure she could do that. Shaken, she moistened her lips with the tip of her tongue. "Could I speak with Mr. Fielding?"

He tapped the pen impatiently. "I'd like to have more information first."

She needed facts, too. Like how Clark could have betrayed her by stealing from her after they had been so intimate. If he had a good reason for taking the car, he could have left a note. Along with her despair, resentment toward him began to brew for putting her in this position.

"What will happen to him?" she asked.

A long column of ashes fell off the lawyer's cigarette and blew off the desk as he opened a manila folder. "Let's see here. He's in violation of his parole. It's his second offense in less than five years. Both felonies. I think we can put him behind bars for eight years."

She couldn't do that to him. Clark had spent the last three years of his life locked away. He had told her he had felt his life slipping away in prison. She couldn't condemn him to that again.

"Mr. Schrems." She looked at him directly for the first time. "I'd like to have some time to think this through. Perhaps I was mistaken."

His tone grew sharp with challenge. "Do you realize that filing a false crime report is also a criminal offense?"

She drew in a deep breath. "That's up to you if you want to press charges against me."

Melinda stared. "Are you out of your mind? I can't believe you're willing to risk so much for someone who stole your car."

Felicity didn't waver. "You have my address if you need to contact me. Good day, Mr. Schrems."

Melinda followed her out into the hall, disapproval in her every step. Felicity ignored her.

"Where are we going?" her friend demanded.

"I want to see Clark. I'll meet you at your car." Without waiting for a reply, she turned and walked away.

It wasn't easy to get into the jail, but now she was determined. Downstairs in a stark lobby, a guard behind glass queried her through a speaker. In response to his questions, she told him she was a lawyer with Holdman, Noyles and Trumbull. She even had one of Stewart Noyles's legal cards to hold up to the television camera to show him.

For one moment, Felicity wondered what her rich, aristocratic grandmother would think if she could see her granddaughter lying her way in to see a criminal. But she was driven to talk to him. Otherwise, she knew, she would never be able to let go of her feelings for Clark.

A door opened and she was escorted down a hallway by a burly guard. Several narrow doors lined one side. The guard stopped at the fourth door and unlocked it.

Felicity stepped into a closetlike room with one chair. Across the center of the room was a waist-high ledge. Above it, a sheet of glass extended to the ceiling. She waited for several minutes, feeling the tension mount as the walls of the small room seemed to close in on her.

Then the door on the opposite wall opened and Clark and a guard entered. His hands were behind his back. She didn't realize he was handcuffed until the guard pulled a chair out for him. Clark looked grim—and wary, like an animal caught in a trap who mistrusts all who come to look at it.

The jailer pushed a button to get out of the room. The door closed behind him with a heavy click, locking Clark in.

Watching him, Felicity felt something catch in her throat and she almost reached toward him. Then she steeled herself. He was here because he had stolen from her.

"I've already talked with the prosecutor," she said bluntly.

Something flickered in his eyes, then died. "Why? I thought you knew me better." Hostility warred with defeat.

"I thought I did, too. I was a fool."

He stiffened, staring at her with impenetrable gray eyes. "Seems we both were."

For a moment, she was caught off guard. Was he saying he had trusted her and he also felt betrayed? Naturally he would try to make her feel the villain.

He would try any trick to convince her she was mistaken. After all, he had a lot to lose; he was facing eight more years in prison.

Still, she had to hear from his lips that he was guilty. "Tell me why I shouldn't press charges," she challenged.

He was silent, watching her as if trying to make up his mind. After a long interval, he said slowly, "No, I don't think I will."

There was more he wasn't saying. She could sense it. But he seemed defiant rather than remorseful. She couldn't be sure if that was genuine hurt in his eyes or if he was an awfully good con.

Rising, she said contemptuously, "I'm not going to press charges, but I want to make one thing clear. I never want to see you again. Ever. I'll put your things in your car. You can come for it tomorrow." She would make a point of not being there.

Pivoting away from him, she started toward the door, determined not to give him the satisfaction of seeing the tears glistening in her eyes. She blinked at them resolutely. A Simmons had more dignity than to cry in public over a man like Clark Fielding.

# Nine

——

Clark felt the metal scrape against his wrists as the handcuffs were removed. He chafed absently at the raw skin as he was processed out of jail. His thoughts were elsewhere.

During those moments in his cell, sitting on that hard, narrow bed, he had thought about Felicity and the soft mattress in her room. He hadn't believed, hadn't *wanted* to believe, that she really thought he had intended to take her car and never return. They had shared too much for her to harbor such suspicions of him. Yet when he came face to face with her, she had been cold and bitter.

Pride had kept him from trying to explain himself. If she didn't have any greater faith in him than that, what was the use? For a time, he had deluded himself into thinking the barriers between them were not so great. But in the end, he was still an untrustworthy ex-con and she heir to a Boston fortune.

Even if he had tried to tell his story, what would she care if Bruce had intended to kill himself? He had seen the sharp, suspicious way she had watched Bruce. His friends could never pass in her world. He had lied to himself in thinking, even for an instant, that *he* could.

At least Bruce was all right. He had been upset when Clark arrived, but he had grown calmer as they talked. He was still worried about finding a job. But he did, as Clark reminded him, have some money until work materialized.

Leaving the police station, Clark walked to the curb and waited for a bus to take him back to Bruce's shabby rented room. His apartment wasn't yet ready and was the only place in the world he had to go to.

After saying goodbye to Melinda, Felicity spent the night in Boston at her grandmother's Beacon Hill house. She arrived late and went straight to bed without telling Gram about the events that had transpired. As she lay in the large bedroom with the pink iris wallpaper that she had picked when she was fifteen, sleep was impossible. She tossed and turned, thinking about Clark and the ordeal at the police station.

She was downstairs for breakfast at seven o'clock, sitting in front of the bow window of the Greek revival house and staring unseeingly out of the mauve-tinted glass, a trademark of the most expensive homes in the city.

Half an hour later, Gram joined her in the stately room with its buff-colored walls and solid Empire furniture. She glanced at Felicity and shook her head. "You look like death warmed over. Are you feeling well?"

"I'm fine," she said listlessly.

The old woman fixed her with a gimlet eye over her Limoges coffee cup. "So you say. I'm curious why you came to Boston on such a spur-of-the-moment visit."

Felicity knew she might as well tell the truth. Her grandmother had always known when she was lying. And the story was bound to get around through Melinda. "Clark Fielding stole my car and drove it to Boston. I came to get it back."

The old woman's chin came up in aristocratic indignation. "Of all the nerve! Not that I'm surprised. I told you from the very beginning that he was not to be trusted."

"I should have listened." Felicity's anger took root. Other people had seen cause to be suspicious of Clark. Why had she been so stupidly gullible?

Her grandmother stabbed a serrated grapefruit spoon into the ripe, pink fruit. "And after you took the time and trouble to help him shop for clothes. He should be ashamed. Did he have anything to say for himself?"

Felicity's mouth tightened. "No." He had not even apologized. In fact, he had had the nerve to look at her with disappointment, as though *she* were the one who had done something wrong.

"That's to be expected, I daresay. Those kind of people never feel guilt or remorse. No doubt he was only sorry that he was caught."

*Those kind of people*, Felicity repeated silently. She had actually thought she and Clark could overcome any barriers between them. In the innermost recesses of her heart, she had begun to think of something fine and lasting forming between them. But they were too different for that to ever have happened, and she had been foolish to have wanted it.

"Perhaps something positive can come from this unpleasant experience," Gram said. "It ought to convince you it's the wisest course to close down the inn."

Felicity looked up sharply. "No. I intend to stay there."

Her grandmother expelled an impatient sigh. "You're being stubborn, child. Your friends are here. All the eligible young men are here. You're wasting your life out there." Pausing, she added her trump card. "And I very much suspect you cannot afford to operate much longer. Am I correct?"

"I can cut some corners, and I'll be fine," Felicity said with more assurance than she felt.

Gram sniffed. "That's up to you, but you know I won't contribute to your mistake by helping you out financially."

"I know." She didn't deny for a minute that money wasn't a worry to her.

She was still worried about finances when she returned to the Cape that afternoon. That and the strain Clark had created in her life made for another long night.

When she was still awake at six the next morning, she decided she might as well get up. It had snowed during the night and the temperature had dropped. Her reaction when her bare feet touched the ice-cold floor in the bathroom was to turn up the heat.

Felicity was in the hall with her hand on the thermostat when she hesitated. Her fuel bill was high enough already. She needed to find ways to keep the heat in instead of producing more.

She had noticed that some people in town put clear plastic over their windows to insulate. In the past, she would have hired a handyman to do such a job for her. Now, however, she decided to do it herself.

Even though it was Clark who had encouraged her to be more self-sufficient, she felt almost defiant toward him as she drove into the hardware store and bought a roll of plastic, strips of wood and nails. She didn't need him to help her. She would manage on her own. If she recognized her belligerence toward him as a way of covering up the ache, she didn't admit it.

With grim purpose, Felicity spent the day nailing up the window covering. It was a cold job, but it went surprisingly well. At times when the wind caught at the plastic and blew it about, it would have been nice to have a helper. But she managed.

In fact, she was feeling proud of herself as she finished the final downstairs windows and went inside for a cup of hot tea. Already she was proving she didn't need Clark. Considering the kind of person he had turned out to be, she was well rid of him.

At least that was what she told herself. But there was an unpleasant queasiness in her stomach that wouldn't go away. And that night Felicity awoke feeling bereft and lonely. She couldn't stop thinking about Clark and how vulnerable he had looked in that stark questioning room, his hands cuffed behind him.

Tossing back the covers, she crossed to the window. The night sky was flecked with bright stars and the path of the moon on the water was white gold. It was a beautiful sight, but it made her sad that she had no one to share it with.

All her life, it seemed, she had been alone. Except for those barely remembered times with her parents, she had never belonged to anyone. Gram was very dear to her, but her grandmother's natural reserve kept a distance between them. With Clark, Felicity had almost built a bridge to another person.

Could she have been so wrong about him? The facts seemed to say no, but her instinct told her yes. What if there were circumstances behind Clark taking the car that she knew nothing about?

A hard gust of wind rattled the window. Shivering in her bare feet, she returned to bed and slipped in between the warm flannel sheets.

"Stop it," she told herself firmly. She was not going to romanticize Clark or try to invent excuses for him. He was a thief and that was that.

She would get over him soon enough.

December came, then Christmas.

The days were long and empty. Felicity's spirits were low. She was restless and moody much of the time. And she had not gotten over Clark. He still occupied far too many of her thoughts, try as she would to put him from her mind.

Felicity closed the inn and went to spend the holidays in Boston with her grandmother. Clark was still in her thoughts even though her days were filled with last-minute shopping and visits to old friends who were in town to be with their families. At nights, there were parties. Some were small get-togethers around fireplaces in historic town houses, others were lavish gatherings glittering with gems and crystal.

Gram insisted on buying Felicity a chic designer gown for the biggest event of the year—the hunt-club ball. The event was being held in the city's best hotel on Christmas Eve.

Gram and Felicity arrived by chauffeured limousine. Snow was falling as she helped her grandmother up the marble steps and into the lobby of the grand old building.

Felicity's white satin gown with its single strand of pearls holding up the right shoulder looked as if it had been designed with her in mind. It showed cleavage and accented curves, falling from her hips into a flowing line. As she surrendered her white satin wrap at the cloakroom and entered the ballroom, she was aware of more than one appraising masculine eye on her.

The theme was "A Victorian Christmas" and the backdrop evoked the mood well. A giant spruce tree stood near the buffet table, twinkling with candles in little tin holders. Antique teddy bears and fragile porcelain dolls rested in tree limbs alongside plaid velvet bows. A child's turn-of-the-century train ran around and around the base of the tree.

Thinking about the children who had once owned these toys made her nostalgic and a little melancholy. Deliberately, she fought back any traces of sadness; she had felt enough of it the past weeks. She was determined not to let it intrude into her time here in Boston. Forcing her gaze from the tree, she looked around the vast room.

Evergreen boughs with matching red bows hung from the elaborate silver wall sconces that dotted the walls and decorated the extravagant crystal chandeliers. At the other end of the room, couples danced to orchestra music. Closer to her, people sat at tables or mingled.

The room was a sea of men in tuxedos and women in long dresses. Young and some not-so-young women wore vibrant, sexy gowns. Older women were dressed in matronly organza and lace. Felicity smiled at several people she recognized.

"There's quite a crowd," she murmured.

"Yes." Gram frowned in the direction of the lavish buffet table. "I do hope the caviar is fresh. Go mingle, dear."

Felicity did, chatting first with an old friend from Vassar and then murmuring over baby pictures with a new mother she knew from Junior League.

Later, she danced with Stewart. He held her in his arms and led her into the waltz with an expert's ease. But she couldn't appreciate his skill. Instead, she kept comparing his touch to Clark's and remembering how breathless she had felt standing so close to him.

After the last strains of the music faded, she thanked him and walked to one of the French doors. Outside, the stone balcony was carpeted with snow. Dimly, she heard chimes from a church holiday service.

Tomorrow was Christmas. Would Clark spend it alone?

She shouldn't worry about him. But she did. Two weeks ago, while writing out Christmas cards, she had even considered sending him one. A wry smile touched her lips at the thought of what Melinda would say to her sending a card to the man who had stolen her car.

"A penny for your thoughts, kid." She looked into the smiling face of Roger Chambers. He was a tall, ungainly man whose unorthodox style and willingness to take risks had made him president of a chain of retail stores.

"I wouldn't sell these thoughts for a million dollars." She had spoken unguardedly, saying what was in her heart. Immediately, she regained her presence of mind. "That's an interesting combination, Roger," she said flippantly. "Blue jeans and a dinner jacket." Tucked casually into his cummerbund were a pack of cigarettes and matches.

He grinned. "If you think *I'm* different from the rest of this crew, you ought to meet Pat Stevenson. That's him stuffing olives in his pocket over at the buffet table."

She glanced at the small, bearded man. "He doesn't look too unusual to me."

"Pat's quite an individualist. He started the Electric Abacus computer-programming company in the back of a fruit market and already he's on *Fortune*'s Five Hundred list."

Her eyebrows went up. "The Electric Abacus," she repeated thoughtfully. That was the company Clark had gone to work for. "I'd like to meet him."

Roger, oblivious to the genteel setting, raised a hand and exuberantly waved Pat over.

A moment later, Felicity was shaking hands with the little man. Pat Stevenson's ready smile put her at ease. She found herself chatting first about the weather, then asking questions about his company.

"I know someone who works there," she said casually. "Clark Fielding."

"Oh, yes. He's the new guy in Software Development." He took an olive from his pocket and popped it in his mouth. "Good fellow. How do you know him?"

"He stayed with me a couple of weeks. At my bed and breakfast," she added hastily.

Roger smirked. "You're blushing, Felicity."

"Interesting that you should mention Clark. His parole officer was in to see me just the other day. Seems his brother has finally convinced the authorities that Clark didn't know he was an accomplice to a crime. Now the brother is petitioning the governor to have Clark exonerated."

She stood paralyzed, trying to absorb his meaning. Was Pat Stevenson saying Clark had been framed? Clark's rueful words of several months ago came back to her. "The first thing I did in prison was tell everyone I met that I wasn't guilty."

"Are you all right, Felicity?" Roger asked. "You look pale."

"N-no, I'm fine." But she wasn't. She felt as if an anvil of guilt had been dropped on her shoulders. Swallowing back a lump, she remembered how stricken she had felt to see him in handcuffs. It had been hard enough on her when she thought he was guilty. But if he had been innocent...

Let's be logical, she told herself sternly. He *had* stolen her car.

"I guess the brother is genuinely sorry, but it's a pity it took so long to clear Clark. It would have done Clark a lot more good three years ago." He took another olive from his pocket and dusted the lint off. "Strange world, isn't it?"

She nodded vaguely, still churning over in her mind how defeated Clark had looked standing behind the glass at the jail. That was the last time she had seen him.

Now she wanted to see him and tell him... what? That she had been wrong. He already knew that. That she was sorry. Perhaps that would make him feel better. Or would she only be doing it to assuage her own guilt?

Beside her, the two men had fallen into a conversation about the stock market and mutual funds. Around her, the room hummed with conversation, but she was lost in a world of her own.

"There you are, Felicity." Gram swept to a dignified halt before her. "It's quite late. Almost midnight. Are you ready to leave?"

"Yes."

She was thankful for the opportunity to escape back to her girlish bedroom where she could think. But no easy solutions came to her. She could send him a card, but what could she possibly say to him? She had a vast experience in writing poetic thank-you notes for dinner parties or weekends in the country. But she had no experience in writing to tell a man she might have misjudged him dreadfully.

Besides, his brother saying that he was innocent didn't prove anything. Still, her gut reaction was to believe that Clark was not a criminal. If she could see him, talk to him, surely there was an explanation for the car.

What weighed most heavily on her mind, however, was the thought Clark had gone to Boston to see a woman while he was living at the inn. By now he might be involved in a full-scale romance. As much as it pained her to think it, any contact from her might be an intrusion. Even if there was no woman in his life, she didn't know how he would respond to her.

The best course, she decided sadly, was to leave things as they stood.

New Year's Day came and went. Felicity returned to the inn. January was bleak and cold. The wind whipped hard out of the north. The house seemed always chilly. And lonely. Snow fell, laying a soft white carpet over the land all the way down to the beach. Looking out the kitchen window, she thought how nice it would be to make fresh tracks in the snow with someone. Or sit inside by a cozy fire together.

If she dwelled too much on such thoughts, though, she became teary-eyed. So she tried not to think about the lonely ache inside.

Instead, she got up each day with a schedule of things to do. She went to the library and checked out an armload of books with titles like *How to be your Own Handyman* and *You Can Fix It Yourself*.

In between teaching piano lessons, she took the books downstairs to the basement and taught herself to identify the tools on the workbench. Within three days, she had learned the names of every item in the metal collection. It gave her a sense of accomplishment to be able to pick up a pipe wrench and know what it was.

Still, except for a professor and his wife who came to spend a weekend, she had no guests and time passed slowly. She was anxious for someone to talk to. When Melinda came to spend a day toward the end of January, Felicity was thrilled.

Over a cup of chamomile tea in the parlor, she proudly showed off her new wisdom. Leaning forward to pass a bone-china plate of coffee cake, she asked, "Do you know the difference between a Phillips screwdriver and a regular screwdriver?"

"Well, they both have vodka and orange juice."

Felicity grinned. "I'm not talking about drinks. They're tools. I've used both of them over the past week. *And* I changed the furnace filter myself. There was really nothing to it." In fact, it was surprising how easy the task had been. To think she had been paying to have it done.

Melinda surveyed her quizzically. "Do you ever think you might be getting a little eccentric out here by yourself?"

A laugh rippled up from Felicity's throat. "Not eccentric—independent, Melinda. And it's a nice feeling." She finished her tea and reached for another piece of coffee cake.

"Of course, there are still lots of things I can't do by myself, but Clark once said—" She stopped. She hadn't meant to speak his name. Now that she had, she felt tense, less carefree.

Melinda, busy stirring sugar into her tea, didn't notice the change in atmosphere. "Whatever happened to him?" she asked.

"He's in Boston working for a computer company."

"You never pressed charges on the car?"

"No."

Melinda sighed. "I didn't think you would. Well, I suppose you know best what you want to do." Rising, she smoothed out the wrinkles of her fashionable dirndl skirt. "What do you say to driving into town to shop? They have such charming little shops here on the Cape."

Felicity faked a bright smile. "That would be pleasant."

"Good. It may be my last chance to do any serious shopping for a while if the weather predictions are accurate. There's supposed to be a real blizzard moving in at the end of the week."

Clark heard the winter storm warnings on the way to work the first day of February. The storm was not predicted to hit Boston hard. But further north and to the east, subzero temperatures, drifting snow and blizzard conditions were expected to make for an ugly situation.

He thought of Felicity up there alone on the Cape while an icy wind battered at the house. Would she be all right?

Jerking the wheel hard to the left, he steered off the interstate, annoyed with himself. Why was he even thinking about her? He was sure she was not wasting her time worrying about him. If the weather got bad, she'd have to sit it out like everyone else.

He parked behind the modern three-building complex that housed management, research and development, and manufacturing for the fast-growing Electric Abacus Company. In spite of the high-tech look of the building, it was run to meet the needs of the individual workers. Some employees didn't even come in; they worked at home, having access to the centralized computer system via home terminals.

He could work at his apartment, too, if he wanted. But it was so depressing, he was always anxious to escape it. Even Bruce's room seemed more homey, and Clark spent a lot of time there, ignoring the parole ban on consorting with former inmates.

Bruce had come a long way in the past couple of months. He had landed a job working part-time for a moving company. It was hard, back-breaking work, but it gave him an enormous sense of satisfaction and had improved his morale tremendously. He was also taking classes to get his high-school diploma and was already talking about college.

Clark took the elevator to his third-floor office. It was a cheery room with bright blue walls and philodendrons growing in glazed pottery vases. He opened the white miniblinds and looked up at the darkening sky.

He really wasn't worried about Felicity, he told himself.

So why did he turn the radio on in his office at ten o'clock to hear the weather? And why did he stiffen in his swivel chair when the announcer said inhabitants of the far end of the Cape were being encouraged to evacuate? The weatherman said the storm was even worse than originally predicted and was bringing with it gale-force winds and waves.

He needed to finish a spread sheet for an accounting program, but he couldn't concentrate.

Rising, he began to pace the small office, walking to the window and fidgeting with the cord of the blind, then pivoting and retracing his steps to the door. Did she have somewhere to go?

Don't worry about her, you fool.

Her grandmother lived in Boston. Surely Felicity would have enough sense to drive down out of the path of such a dangerous storm.

Don't worry about her, he told himself.

Abandoning his computer terminal, he again paced to the window. The sky was dark and ominous-looking toward the north.

Felicity wouldn't leave, he thought with heavy resignation. She would stay with the house.

If the storm knocked down the fragile electric lines, she would be without heat and light. She might be stranded for several days before help could reach her.

He made himself sit down and try to be calm. Cape Cod was not an isolated spot in the mountains or some remote jungle. It was near the center of civilization. Surely she would be all right.

# Ten

———

The snow came in fierce gusts, driven by the raw, seaborne wind. Felicity stood by the window and watched the big flakes fall, hugging her arms tightly around herself against the chill.

The weather reports were full of news of an approaching storm. Harsh weather in winter was not uncommon, but this was going to be a particularly bad one. The announcer even advised going inland until the front passed.

She thought about it. She packed a bag and set it by the door. But she didn't leave.

Gram called at noon. "You *are* coming into Boston, aren't you? You must have heard they're predicting a terrible storm up on the Cape.''

Felicity looked out the parlor window. The snow was drifted up to the windowsills, constantly shifting as the restless wind changed directions.

"I've heard. But it seems to me driving on icy roads would be as dangerous as staying here in a well-built building and waiting for the storm to pass.''

Gram hesitated. "Well, you may have a point.''

Although Felicity couldn't have expressed it as easily, something else held her to the house. It was all she had, and she couldn't bring herself to abandon it easily. She would rather be here than sitting in Boston worrying about it.

"On the other hand—''

"It's still early, Gram. I have a bag packed, and I'm ready to go at a moment's notice if the need arises.''

"Very well." Her grandmother didn't sound happy, but she'd capitulated.

By two in the afternoon, Felicity had begun to question her decision. Standing in the dining room, she peeked out the lace curtains. It looked like dusk outside. The angry snow clouds were iron gray in color, their very weight seeming to pull them lower in the sky. The wind slapped the house like an angry creature until most of the plastic was ripped from the windows and blowing in shreds.

She could still leave. But she cringed at the thought of driving across the bridge over the canal that connected the Cape to the mainland. With winds this high, it seemed safer to take her chances in a substantial old house than in a fragile car that might be swept off the road into the icy water.

She had been through storms before, but this was shaping up to be the worst in her experience. The wind was as wild as she had ever heard it. Felicity had the creepy sensation it was a menacing, living thing lurking in wait outside the house. With a shiver, she dropped the curtain and moved away from the window.

"You're getting fanciful," she told herself. A cup of hot tea would cure that.

But as she sat at the oval table in the dining room drinking tea, a shutter ripped loose upstairs and began banging against the side of the house. The noise unnerved her, especially since the sky loomed ever darker.

By five o'clock, it was as dark as the middle of the night outside. She turned on every light in the house and put on soothing classical music. But the music was often overshadowed by the eerie howling of the wind.

Edgy and restless, Felicity closed all the curtains. It was going to be a long night. She tried to watch television but the antenna must have been knocked down, and she couldn't pick up any stations. After half an hour, she gave up trying to interest herself in a book.

At nine, she went upstairs to bed, but the storm raging outside made sleep impossible. After listening to branches snapping off trees and the sound of the loose shutter banging, she tossed back the covers and went to look out the window.

The wind blew even harder, making the huge panes of glass flex in and out. She watched with a mixture of fascination and fright. If the glass bulged any farther, it would surely break.

As if thinking it had made it happen, she heard a snapping noise. While she stared in horror, a jagged line ran diagonally across the window. For one breathless moment, the glass remained in place. Then it shattered and crumpled, falling to the ground a story below. She was left standing in the dark with wet snow pelting in on her.

"Be calm," she told herself, but an edge of panic rose up in her throat as she turned and made her way across to the wall light switch.

No lights came on when she flipped the switch. The electricity was out. Standing in the cold darkness, she knew there was not a soul around for miles.

Felicity had never felt so alone and frightened in her life.

The big house was black and seemed ominously empty when Clark pushed his way through the heavy front door. He had to struggle to close it while the wind fought him.

"Felicity!"

No answer.

He didn't know whether to be worried or relieved. If she wasn't here, then he had been a fool to risk his life to get here. But she had to be here; her car was outside. Besides, he had spoken to her grandmother at two o'clock, and she had said Felicity intended to stay.

The old woman had been worried enough to actually confide that she had been trying to call for the past hour and couldn't get through. Apparently Felicity's phone was dead. Mrs. Simmons was clearly anxious. So was he.

Clark had spent the last eight hours making his way along a deserted highway that often dead-ended in banks of drifting snow. Fortunately, he had been able to drive off the road and around the drifts on the frozen ground. Big limbs that had been broken off trees scuttled across the slick road. It had been a slow, nerve-racking trip and more than once he had feared the wind would turn his car over. But he had made it. Now, where the hell was she?

"Felicity," he called again.

Snapping on a flashlight, he started through the house. The first place he checked was her bedroom. It was freezing. No wonder, with the window broken. That scared him. Uneasy, he checked the other rooms, then went down to the ground floor. She wasn't there, either.

With a quickening of apprehension, he descended into the basement and opened a door at the bottom of the stairs. There, standing in a halo of light from a kerosene lamp, stood Felicity. Behind her on the wooden shelves of what was clearly an old fruit cellar, he saw several fresh cans of vegetables, a propane camp stove and a stack of blankets. She stood in front of an army cot holding a steaming cup, filled with tea, no doubt, in both hands.

He felt suddenly ridiculous for risking his neck to get here. She didn't need him; she obviously had everything under control—right down to the tea.

But when she put the cup down and moved a step closer, he saw that her chin was beginning to quiver. "Clark," she said in a breaking voice. She lifted her hands toward him, like a child pleading to be held.

He stepped quickly closer and pulled her against him, feeling the supple fragility of her body. The pure relief of being able to touch her brought a lump to his throat. Felicity felt the same emotion.

"Are you all right?" he asked thickly.

She nodded. Gulping back tears, she buried her face against his shoulder. "I—I'm so glad you're here." Wrapping her arms around his waist, she clung tightly, almost overcome by the need to assure herself he was real and not a mirage she had conjured up because she wanted him so badly. She had the irrational fear if she didn't hold on hard enough, he would be snatched away from her.

The last few hours had been the loneliest, hardest time she had ever spent. Seeing anyone would have been a solace, but she was immeasurably thankful it was Clark. Knowing that he had braved hours of hellish driving to make sure she was safe brought more tears to her eyes. A sob broke past the constriction in her throat.

He brushed back her disheveled hair with gentle hands. "Hush, honey. It's okay now. Don't cry."

"Just hold me," she managed to whisper.

He did, clutching her so closely she felt the wild thudding of his heart and the sinewed strength of his body. She heard him swallow and knew he was as moved as she.

Then she looked up into his eyes and saw they were moist with tenderness. Slowly, she lifted her mouth to his and their lips met in a kiss almost chaste in its purity. She recognized passion waiting beneath the surface as his lips caressed hers, but she also read reverence and a sense of awe. This was a mating of souls that expressed more than a barrage of words ever could. Recognizing that moved her in a way that nothing else could have. Now the tears that escaped her were ones of raw emotion.

Finally they drew apart.

Clark reached into his pocket and pulled out a handkerchief. He began wiping the wetness from her

cheeks with careful strokes. Looking down through
eyelashes beaded with teardrops, Felicity could see
the calluses on his hands.

Everything about him seemed very dear to her.
The fact he had come told her many things that
words couldn't adequately convey. He cared about
her in ways far deeper than she had allowed herself
to believe. And she cared as much for him.

He fitted his big hands more securely around her
slender waist. When he spoke, his voice was full of
emotion. "I was so worried about you."

"I'm okay," she said shakily. "It didn't at first
occur to me to come down into the basement, but I
asked myself what you would have done."

He pulled her closer. "Good girl."

Felicity nestled her head against his shoulder and
they clung together again in silence. She didn't know
how long they remained like that. The moments kept
getting lost in time. But it was long enough for her to
be satisfied that this was real and to feel the wet snow
of his coat rubbing her cheek and to inhale the scent
of after-shave. She felt freed, born again. A sound
that was half sob, half laugh escaped her.

He put his hands on her shoulders and pushed her
back enough to look down at her.

Her voice wispy with wonder, she said, "To think
I had visions of making you into a carbon copy of
the men I knew in Boston."

He watched her with puzzled eyes, waiting for her to continue.

"I was going to change you. Instead, you changed me." As his expression turned to concern, she said hastily, "Oh, I don't mean that in a bad way. I had always relied on other people to fix things for me, and I wasn't confident about being able to take care of things. You taught me to rely on myself."

She attempted a watery smile and saw an answering softening in his eyes. "You even yelled at me. I remember thinking that Stewart would never do that."

"I know I'm not like this guy Stewart," he admitted, "but—"

"Hush." She put a finger on his lips to silence him. "No, you're not like Stewart. And I'm grateful for that. Stewart didn't come all the way from Boston in this weather because he was worried about me. But you did."

A smile of relief formed. "I'm glad you feel that way. I wasn't sure how you would react to seeing me. All during the drive I went back and forth between feeling foolish for coming and being sorry I hadn't left sooner."

"I know what you mean." She pulled off his wet gloves and rubbed his hands between hers. It felt good to touch him, to be near him without any undercurrents of uncertainty between them. "I've felt the same confusion since you left. I've had a thousand regrets about how things ended between us. I can't count the times I've started to write to you but I was afraid to."

"It was a pretty traumatic parting," he agreed grimly. He drew away to take off his heavy winter coat.

"It was my fault. I jumped to conclusions when I shouldn't have. If I had asked you instead of accusing you when you were standing behind that plate-glass partition at the jail, I know you would have explained what happened. Or if I had simply trusted you—" She broke off unhappily, full of regret.

He lifted his shoulders in a regretful shrug. "My pride was hurt. But I owed you an explanation."

"No, you didn't," she insisted.

"Yes, I did."

Her smile cut through the tension. "Surely we aren't going to argue?"

"No, we're not," he agreed, pulling her toward him. "We should be lovers, not fighters."

"Lovers," she repeated softly.

He had carried her once before—the night she had drunk too much wine. She had been too giddy then to notice details. But this time, when he put a strong arm behind the backs of her knees and another around her back, she felt the seasoned lines of his body and the hard strength of him. He picked up the flashlight with an easy, swooping motion and headed up the stairs.

The wind was still strong outside, but Felicity paid little attention to it. It no longer seemed like a threat. Nothing worried her now that Clark was here.

He carried her up the second flight of stairs without ever slowing down. Then they were in his bedroom. She thought he would put her on the brass bed. Instead, he laid her on the floor.

"I liked this carpet from the minute I stepped into this room. It will feel good against your bare skin," he promised huskily.

He was right. But what felt even better against her was *his* bare skin. His hungry kisses and wandering hands and sharp sighs mingled with her own to transport her to a paradise of senses.

The beam of the flashlight hit against the ceiling to form a halo of light above them. Ribbons of silver traced along the walls.

They kissed as she had not known it could be—deeply, intimately, all-consuming until she was shivery under the stroking of his tongue. Her hands roamed over the tightly knit muscles of his shoulders and chest and stomach and the softer recesses of his inner thighs. There was nowhere she did not feel free to touch.

While his mouth continued to dip into hers, he filled her with the strength of his love.

The moments that followed were wrapped in the gauzy tissue of passion. Under his caresses, she ascended to trembling heights until, for one breathless

moment, she was perched atop a pinnacle of ec-
stasy. Then she tumbled down the other side.

Felicity opened her eyes to the darkness and smiled
tremulously.

For a moment the only sound was their ragged
breathing. Then Clark said quietly, "I can't imagine
ever not being able to do this with you."

She opened her eyes and smiled into his. "I want
that, too," she said. In fact, she had taken it as a
given, so she didn't immediately understand the hesitation in his voice.

He ran a hand through his hair. "But I'm not sure
your grandmother would ever approve of me."

"She doesn't approve of me running the inn,
either." Slowly, she explained, "I love Gram, but I
have to make my own choices. Besides, I think it will
go a long way with her that you showed so much
concern for me."

"Then you'd marry me?"

"Yes," she said breathlessly.

He pulled her back against his bare chest, whis-
pering soft words of endearment into her ear.

For long moments she snuggled against him,
marveling in the fact they were together. Only when
a thought occurred to her did she frown slightly.
"What would happen to the inn? I mean, would we
have to close it and move to Boston?"

He raised up on one elbow and looked down at
her, stroking the filaments of silken hair from her

face as he spoke. "I don't see why. I can write software programs anywhere if I have a computer terminal. I would only have to go into the office occasionally."

Relieved, she pressed a kiss on his bare shoulder. "I'm glad. I would like to stay here."

"I like that idea, too," he said.

"We have so much more to teach each other—a lifetime's worth—and this house will be a wonderful place to do it in."

\*   \*   \*   \*   \*

**For the millions who can't read
Give the Gift of Literacy**

One out of five adults in North America
cannot read or write well enough
to fill out a job application
or understand the directions on a bottle of medicine.

**You can change all this by joining the fight
against illiteracy.**

For more information write to:
Contact, Box 81826, Lincoln, Neb. 68501
In the United States, call toll free: 1-800-228-8813

**The only degree you need
is a degree of caring**

# Take 4 Silhouette Special Edition novels
# and a surprise gift
# FREE

Then preview 6 brand-new books—delivered to your door as soon as they come off the presses! If you decide to keep them, you pay just $2.49 each*—a 9% saving off the retail price, *with no additional charges for postage and handling!*

Romance is alive, well and flourishing in the moving love stories of Silhouette Special Edition novels. They'll awaken your desires, enliven your senses and leave you tingling all over with excitement.

Start with 4 Silhouette Special Edition novels and a surprise gift absolutely FREE. They're yours to keep without obligation. You can always return a shipment and cancel at any time.

Simply fill out and return the coupon today!

\* Plus 69¢ postage and handling per shipment in Canada.

## *Silhouette Special Edition*®

# BY DEBBIE MACOMBER....

**ONCE UPON A TIME,** in a land not so far away, there lived a girl, Debbie Macomber, who grew up dreaming of castles, white knights and princes on fiery steeds. Her family was an ordinary one with a mother and father and one wicked brother, who sold copies of her diary to all the boys in her junior high class.

One day, when Debbie was only nineteen, a handsome electrician drove by in a shiny black convertible. Now Debbie knew a prince when she saw one, and before long they lived in a two-bedroom cottage surrounded by a white picket fence.

As often happens when a damsel fair meets her prince charming, children followed, and soon the two-bedroom cottage became a four-bedroom castle. The kingdom flourished and prospered, and between soccer games and car pools, ballet classes and clarinet lessons, Debbie thought about love and enchantment and the magic of romance.

One day Debbie said, ''What this country needs is a good fairy tale.'' She remembered how well her diary had sold and she dreamed again of castles, white knights and princes on fiery steeds. And so the stories of Cinderella, Beauty and the Beast, and Snow White were reborn....

---

Look for Debbie Macomber's *Legendary Lovers* trilogy from Silhouette Romance: *Cindy and the Prince* (January, 1988); *Some Kind of Wonderful* (March, 1988); *Almost Paradise* (May, 1988). Don't miss them!

 *Silhouette Desire*

# COMING
# NEXT MONTH

**#397 TO LOVE AGAIN—Lass Small**
After a personal tragedy, Felicia's feelings were totally numb—and she intended to keep them that way. But Nate wasn't about to let a will of steel come between him and the woman he loved.

**#398 WEATHERING THE STORM—Elaine Camp**
Simon wanted no part of the past he'd shared with Marlee. But she had a foolproof plan to change his mind. Simon was no fool, and he found that together they could weather any storm.

**#399 TO THE HIGHEST BIDDER—Cathryn Clare**
Thrown together over possession of a New England farmhouse, Janni and Bart planned to battle it out. Though the house was collateral, they found they couldn't put a price on love.

**#400 LIGHTNING STRIKES TWICE—Jane Gentry**
Dr. Jake Rowan was back, but Attorney Nola O'Brien wasn't interested. He'd left her heartbroken, but now he was determined to right past wrongs—the answer was love!

**#401 BUILT TO LAST—Laurel Evans**
Pressures from her job had Allison Napoli looking for an alternative life-style, and architect Josh Fitzpatrick was just the answer. But could he convince her that home was where the heart is?

**#402 INDISCREET—Tess Marlowe**
When Terri Genetti was forced to close her business, she didn't know handsome entrepreneur Jim Holbrook was behind her problems. But Terri learned she could follow her heart without betraying her dreams.

---

# AVAILABLE NOW:

**#391 BETRAYED BY LOVE**
Diana Palmer

**#392 RUFFLED FEATHERS**
Katherine Granger

**#393 A LUCKY STREAK**
Raye Morgan

**#394 A TASTE OF FREEDOM**
Candice Adams

**#395 PLAYING WITH MATCHES**
Ariel Berk

**#396 TWICE IN A LIFETIME**
BJ James

In response
to last year's outstanding success,
Silhouette Brings You:

# Silhouette Christmas Stories 1987

Specially chosen for you in a delightful volume celebrating the holiday season, four original romantic stories written by four of your favorite Silhouette authors.

Dixie Browning—*Henry the Ninth*
Ginna Gray—*Season of Miracles*
Linda Howard—*Bluebird Winter*
Diana Palmer—*The Humbug Man*

Each of these bestselling authors will enchant you with their unforgettable stories, exuding the magic of Christmas and the wonder of falling in love.

A heartwarming Christmas gift during the holiday season...indulge yourself and give this book to a special friend!

## Available now

XM87-1R